MW01536468

The Timeman

Amo Sulaiman

PublishAmerica

Baltimore

© 2003 by Amo Sulaiman.
All rights reserved. No part of this book may be reproduced in any form without written permission from the publishers, except by a reviewer who may quote brief passages in a review to be printed in a newspaper or magazine.

First printing

ISBN: 1-59286-800-2
PUBLISHED BY PUBLISHAMERICA BOOK PUBLISHERS
www.publishamerica.com
Baltimore

Printed in the United States of America

DEDICATION

To Michelle and Marc and their cousins

Those who can make you believe absurdities can make you commit atrocities.
Voltaire

Preface

I'm Scott Bowman; everyone calls me Scotty in Sandreef. I used to have a public image when I was an alcoholic and homeless. I was an inoffensive outcast in my own community, especially to newcomers. I still believe that all of my problems started when I experienced my first trance—a state of being completely absent from my surroundings and myself. Though I used to be in a lifeless standing position during my trances, you shouldn't think about those unconscious spells as epileptic seizures. My body remained stiffer than a stale corpse without manifesting other symptoms.

To deal with my trances, I started drinking until that couldn't repair the damage done to my family and me. My wife and children abandoned their misery and the terrible situations that I had condemned them to endure by leaving me nine years ago. You might be thinking that I'm still suffering from the old ways of my life. You are right. My past still makes my hands tremble. It is natural to think that I am very odd, and isn't it especially odd that my trances caused me to become an alcoholic? To answer that question and to come to terms with myself, I am compelled to share the nature of my trances with you.

In my trances, I was always paralyzed and mentally blocked. Each spell that I experienced lasted exactly four hours. Sometimes, I had more than one trance a day. Though I had suffered from these trances for years until the very day that everything I had witnessed in my dream-like world actually happened , the contents of my trances never changed. It was like looking at the same movie over and over again without the power to alter its flow. I was also a privileged observer who couldn't change the direction of what I perceived. To a certain extent others' thoughts appeared clear to me. But when it came to the Timeman, I couldn't go beyond his coarse voice. The peculiar part of it all is that I had a role in it. I was an actor, too, and it was like reading about myself from a written script. But my role was less interesting compared to Mr Cougar's and Edwin's bitter struggles and confrontations against the Timeman. Their conflict was about life, death, the principle of the soul, and the meaning of time. All this is linked to morality in society.

The most amazing part is that everyone in our community believes that they have always known Mr Ralph Cougar and his grandson Edwin very well. But this is far from the truth, for I saw their hidden nature in my trances. But I didn't warn them about their future. I couldn't bring the contents of my spell to consciousness without going more insane. How could I speak about such experiences? My community already believed that I was crazy, so revealing anything about my trances would be telling them that I was completely insane. Also, it was like my tongue was tied, and I couldn't utter my experiences to myself. I was the first victim of my own trances. Other victims stumbled in their paths when they heard about the Timeman's inescapable cell. This would make any sane person give up his beliefs about an afterlife.

Besides the upfront conflicts between Mr Cougar, the Timeman, and Edwin, Mr Cougar appears to me as a social philosopher who teaches us about social morality. He argues this view on the basis of the principle of the soul as a community soul. Along with the nature of the soul, he includes the significance of death in his teaching. But the Timeman sees the mind or soul as a useless entity after death because the body cannot interact with it to bring about any relevant changes.

S.B.

12:00 Commanding Death

'A picture of sadness you are! Against a treacherous and disloyal vermin like you, graveyards scorn at a deteriorating shadow on the wall. Escape me you can't! Never will you run away from me! Your eternal master I am! Hide in a pit of abolition; I'll get you. I'll suck you up and swallow you like a slimy worm and spit you out all decomposed! Your destiny, your doom, you're up against.' The cold voice rang within Mr Cougar. It sounded as though doom had cried out to him.

'What? What's this?' questioned Mr Cougar, for this had been the strangest thing he'd ever experienced. He'd been taken in by this horrible male voice, and it had been too vivid to be a hallucination. He was sweating, for that bad-tempered creature could burn the most sensitive rose bush.

Mr Cougar's eyebrows tightened; they struggled to view the tormentor; they searched the horizon for a sign, but the sky was too blue to show an impression. 'My dear tormentor, reveal yourself. You've entered into my mind and taken grip of me without my permission. You've made me so transparent. Show yourself! I don't know you.' All of this crossed his subconscious.

'Graves tremble in my path! Look, at the face of the ultimate destiny maker!'

'You must be very arrogant. Evil and wicked, too. So much anger and hate live in your voice,' Mr Cougar unconsciously replied. For surely the intruder that occupied his mind did not come from a charitable organization; that voice implied that he sought to conquer and obtain ultimate victory over all living things.

9

Mr Cougar continued to wait for the tormentor's facial impressions. 'Now, a patch of cloud is moving in. It's getting bigger, much bigger. It's flattening itself out smoothly. It's opening itself up! In the center, a trace of a face is coming out, all white. It looks colder than crystallized ice. The head is forming, two eye sockets, a concave nose, optimistic lips, the forehead showing no lines. Long wavy hair from his head passes his shoulder. His beard, thick as ever, stretches downward too. Oh no, he's purely white, much whiter than a polar bear. His eyes are still closed. That face, dryer than limestone, is colder and older than the arctic tundra. All the horrors in life mold that frozen face. The image in the sky is undoing itself, receding further and further away. It's screaming out; timelessness is the prize for living. From the glacier, it must have come from. What a petrifying face. Nobody would ever want to confront such an awful monster in his life, not even in the grave. Good gracious, it's going away.'

Mr Cougar believed that the face also had deep blue eyes to match its icy nature. As the image's features and form disappeared from his mind, his soul felt heavier until it tickled his spine in fear.

His subconscious could not totally shake away dreadfulness in itself, for nothing could be scarier than the tormentor's voice: 'It's too alive. Is it really that evil? It would have to boast about being the spirit of all things. If so, I have to be his victim! Why me? I've never done anything wrong to anyone!'

'I, the Timeman, live in all eternity,' cried the voice again.

Mr Cougar's entire life flashed before him incoherently, apparently for something that he might have done; but he had never hurt anybody. And it was not in his nature to harm anyone. He had lived together with others.

'My life is a community,' he said subconsciously. 'It's the deepest meaning of my life. Each person has his little community. I wanted to be understood and for others to be sympathetic to my feelings. It's a necessity for me to live by. Others shape me, too. Just being with others burns my little bulb. Nobody can remove my community, my way of life. I don't try to hide the community from others, and I don't steal from myself. Without community, I'd be a pretentious ghost. I give people enough time to get near me, and I don't deny a person because of bad experiences. I can't hide anything. My community can't be hidden. How could I hide my own happiness or sorrow? I accept myself like a community. And people around me mold me into who I am. They make me genuine, and free to always be lovable. I'm part of their community. And they're part of mine. How could I fulfill my life without living in my community? I never try to remove the happiness of my life – the community!'

It appeared as though the Timeman had receded and was reflecting a little. He knew that reality was raw like an ocean and vulgar like an erupting volcano. And human beings have always fashioned a romantic package for the brute in nature. He opened a time cell and saw Socrates preaching to Criso that *He wouldn't know him after his death because the soul is immaterial and a complete entity in itself. It is pure and eternal. The body can't interact with it because it is independent from the body. The body is a different substance that perished.* He wanted to show Mr Cougar that both the body and soul obeyed his nature of time. The spirits of human beings have been trapped in his time cell. And Mr Cougar wanted to liberate those souls.

'A disloyal beast, you are against traditional meanings of the body and soul, too. How absurd that the soul is a product of one's deed. A community keeps it existing after death,' said the Timeman. 'You believe that your soul exists as long as members in your community remember you. Had you been wicked, people wouldn't want to remember you or your deeds. Your beliefs about the human soul, death, and life are irrational. You would have problems convincing others that their soul is really a community object in which they live. But my nature couldn't be anymore real than it has been for all living things. From a person's birth to his death, I register it chronologically over a period of time. And I preserve the last impression of a person's life. Remember, the soul doesn't have a life span of its own after the body passes away.' All this made Mr Cougar very nervous because he couldn't hide his thoughts from the Timeman.

Because of Mr Cougar's wisdom of community, he had not

foreseen the nightmare standing majestically in his path. Then he thought that he had to be humble to that wretched creature that possessed his mind.

'O, please! Show some kindness, compassion, and mercy. Please, I beg you. Let me go. I'm so old. I live my life fully. Look at me! My toenails are so black and shaky. Nothing whatsoever could hold 'em on my bare skin. Nothing could restore my biscuit skin. My legs have nothing on them. They're full of wrinkles and rough cracks. You can see my bones through my thin onionskin. I'm nothing more than a dried up bamboo, cracking and screeching for help. My stomach touches my backbone. You can see my ribcage through my shit. It hides nothing. My spineless back is worsening each moment. My head reaches my knees when I walk. My arms could sweep the ground these days. Please, sir Timeman! Have some mercy for me. Let me go. I'm already half covered with a white sheet,' begged Mr Cougar, lying on his back in bed like a straightened out paraplegic. His toes bulged out from the bed sheet; his ribs could not really be counted. His thin neck and face remained uncovered. His closed eyes could not stop tears from running along his cheekbone. The warmth of a hand cresting his quickly brought him back to consciousness, but it did not remove the inner interrogator. Mr Cougar's eyes opened wide; fear lived in them.

There was pure malice in the Timeman, especially when he attended to Mr Cougar's body. The Timeman had to show him that the body obeys our common sense view of time. And the mind or soul is a collection of mental activities, thinking, believing, remembering, willing, wanting, etc, but not community soul. Though everybody ages regularly with respect to time, the Timeman wanted to change this for Mr Cougar. His body would obey a different flow of time and age rapidly. He wanted to undermine Mr Cougar's beliefs of the soul. Because only time could be real in any conceived domain.

Mr Cougar was just fifty-three years old and waiting for his death to take him away from all that was enjoyable. He had been a successful fisherman in his little fishing community of Sandreef. It sat on the Northeast Atlantic coast of Newfoundland, Canada.

All this could be found in Sandreef: about two hundred and fifty inhabitants; one school for most ages; a general community health center for humans and non-humans (In some exceptional cases flowers were treated.); two restaurants that served alcohol; a general grocery store; a gas station; a bank; a tailor; a butcher; a hairdresser; a shoe repair; a church; and many fishing boats. Most people had single houses, but a handful of apartment buildings had been thrown up here and there. Everyone was satisfied with living a simple life that harmonized with fishing activities. Whatever the residents could not get there was available in nearby communities. Some students went to high school in the town of Rose Hall, and they did not mind traveling eight kilometers in any weather by school bus or moped.

Time went by, and the community hardly changed; it still sits today on the back of time to remind us of the meaning of life. Nobody deliberately tried to out-fish another, and the desire to relocate to another place hardly ever came with the tide. Daily work stress was alien, and people did not have enough time for it. The daily tide anchored them. Aside from having modern household appliances, people did not rely so much on high-tech equipment. They went out at dawn to set their nets and collected them in the morning when the tide drifted away, leaving its fruits behind to groom communal life. With their catches in hand, they went about their morning programs until the fish truck came about midday to pick up the morning catch. Only on Saturday evenings and Sunday mornings did the fishing boats rest at the harbor. On those days, families strolled along harmoniously, greeted everyone causally, had picnics with neighbors and relatives, and aimlessly walked to other communities to visit old friends and relatives.

Mr Cougar had two married daughters, Betty Sanders and Catherine Morris. The older daughter, Betty, lived several streets away. She and her husband were schoolteachers. They had one teenager son who was very lazy for his age. The younger daughter, Catherine, stayed with him, and she had three children. Mr Cougar lived on the ground floor, with Catherine on the upper floor. Since his wife died six months ago, Catherine had been cooking for him until this very day. This day was much more than special, for nothing like it had ever happened in Sandreef.

At twelve o'clock, on September 10, Mr Cougar told Catherine to invite his sister, all of his close friends, some neighbors, and Betty's family members, because he would die at exactly four o'clock in the afternoon. At twelve o'clock, before his subconscious spell with the Timeman, he had announced his forthcoming death to her. Catherine had hoped that he was really saying something else because he appeared to be dozing on and off with fatigue. Then he repeated it slowly to her; she heard it and thought that it was a tasteless joke, or a hallucination. As he repeated it once again, eye contact with him said it all to her. But she quickly regained her senses and blamed it all on her restless nights with her son, Edwin. Without questioning and doubting her father directly, she checked his forehead for fever and tested his consciousness by having him count fingers; he passed these tests. She was thinking about how unbearable this situation was, and how it could rip anyone's stomach wide open. The cruelty was that everyone would take her father to be a mental case. It would be around the whole community in a jiffy. There would be endless torment and embarrassment. She and her children would have to endure psychological abuse for the rest of their lives; she would not be able to walk in the street with her head up. At the grocery store nothing would stop the gossip and giggling. Her children would become a laughing stock; the teasing would never stop, and they would be insulted by others' dirty looks. They would constantly be asked if their grandpa had died yet. They would not be able to fight an upstream battle for long; it would gradually swallow up their strength, making them only weaklings and nervous wrecks. She knew that if she believed her father, she would commit atrocities against herself and her entire family.

Catherine searched the walls in his room for an answer. His room was confusing: too tidy, and this was totally unusual. She glanced at him and thought that he remained in his room as though he was waiting for someone; she got up and decided to walk about his apartment. She remarked that she had never done this before, at least, intentionally. She went to the bathroom first. Everything was in order, for he had shaved early in the morning, taken a bath, cleaned the washroom, placed every single item in its appropriate place, and emptied the little garbage can. The little kitchen had hardly been used for several months, except for the kettle and bread toaster for quick snacks. He had eaten his breakfast and left the empty containers in the tray on the kitchen table. She went to the living room for a closer look. Unbelievably, the carpet appeared to have been vacuumed that morning. The furniture was free of dust, and a window was half open for fresh air. She had seen enough. Everything had been too well planned, so she went back to his room and stood near the door contemplating his face and thick blond hair that he'd recently had cut. 'Do you want your dinner in bed, dad?'

'Leave it as usual, please. Hurry up! I'd like to say good-bye to my dearest ones and friends,' he murmured.

'Hurry up? This isn't a game! How can you play with people's feelings like this?' she shouted angrily as an out right refusal of his request.

All this time the Timeman had noticed Catherine. She was in shock. It prevented her from having an intellectual insight into her father's revelation of life, death, and the soul. It would have been much more profitable had she asked her father about death, the nature of the soul, and the essence of living. And how he had acquired the knowledge of his coming death. Unfortunately, Catherine couldn't surpass her own feelings at seeing the crumbling of her own life. Catherine went upstairs hastily, using the inside steps of the house, which they had often used during the last six months. Suddenly, she waited for a moment in front of the door.

'Come with me!' the Timeman commanded, expecting Mr Cougar to heed his command.

'Sorry, I'm staying here, in bed,' he replied, looking more scared than before.

'The lord of time stands before you. Be humble to your ultimate superior. Serve me with nobility and reverence. For time and space, I fuse at will. Now, the true Ralph, obey your master command and come forth. Leave that deteriorating body down there, with its primitive instincts to survive.' From Mr Cougar's body, a ghost like image slowly squeezed itself out of the body. The phantom floated to the stairs and then turned back, staring at the body on the bed that couldn't hide the horror on its face.

'Remember, I'm as much you as you are me,' the phantom said to the body in bed.

'You've already abused the privilege I have entrusted upon you,' interrupted the Timeman.

'What manner of sorcery are you practicing?' asked the phantom.

'Sorcery, no. I've only widened the separation between your higher and lower levels of consciousness. And you're the true Ralph. You possess a higher level of thought. You could think much clearer without vulgar emotions clouding your rationality. The lower level is with the lump in the bed. It could response to its surrounding with its sense organs. I hate this part of you. I would allow it to suffer the consequences of another dimension of time.'

'Do you mean to tell me that my higher and lower levels of consciousness would occupy two different time cells? And that they would only interact occasionally with each other?' asked the phantom of Mr Cougar. 'Now, I could really enjoy pure rationality - willingness, organizing, analyzing, thinking, and reflecting without any emotions and physical needs.'

'Yes, I've made the barrier of time much more explicit in you. And since you're too cheeky, I'll cast you into a time cell. You'll exist a moment earlier, so you can't influence and interact with what you observe around you.' Instantaneously, Mr Cougar was locked up in a future time cell without his knowledge and in an imaginary body.

'Why are you torturing me like this?' asked the body in bed. Although the Timeman and the phantom Mr Cougar heard him, no answer came forth.

'Know this, you and that lump there have one source – the body,' he said to Ralph. 'Now you can experience what death and soul are in the realm of time without being choked up with unfounded fear and anger.'

'You meant to say I'm like a soulless ghost that couldn't change the direction of a feather in the wind. And it is impossible for me to escape from your gruesome time cell. So I'm in an analogous situation living in the present without being able to change the past. Now, I'm sitting helplessly in the future and looking down at all that is presently happening in the world,' enquired Mr Cougar, trying to touch and speak to Catherine who was entering her apartment.

'What are you doing?' the Timeman asked. 'If you're in such a hurry to know how miserable you have made others lives, I won't stop you.' Mr Cougar waited and said:

'I really don't have a body. I'm immaterial. I can hear and see without my body!'

'Yes, you perceive with your essence while your body and its bodily consciousness rots in my warp. And don't tell me that you're discontented with your reflective nature. It can't experience the bodily sensations of warmth, cold, pleasure, or pain.'

'Timeman, am I purely soul? An immaterial substance that could live eternally without any pain or pleasure?'

'No, I told you that you're the essence of your existence, observing reflectively. There isn't any soul, only time. I'm the keeper of all. I give each person a unique identity after death. I lock up each person's last impression in a unique time cell. Enjoy the privilege I bestow upon you to roam in the present.' Mr Cougar tried to say something into Catherine's ear without being able to evoke her attention.

'No, Ralph!' interrupted the Timeman, 'You don't exist in her reality.'

'How else should I confirm my new identity? I can walk through everything. I touched her shoulder and nothing happened. I shouted in her ear, but she couldn't hear me. I'm a powerless benevolent spirit without any form. But you see me as having layers of consciousness. Isn't the highest level of consciousness in me about my community soul?'

The Timeman took his time replying.

'Will you observe what you have done to your family with your childish idea of death?' cried the Timeman, witnessing the scene in the living room.

12:15 Catherine's Shock and Fear

Catherine's face wore deep sorrow and profound confusion. She went to the dining room where her family was eating dinner and walked around the dining table serving everyone mashed potato without waiting for requests. She looked for the family member who would be receptive to her speaking, but she did not find one, so she went to the sink to prepare water for the dishes. She washed her hands over and over again, attempting to remove the horrible request of her father.

'Are you going to eat with us, Mom?' asked Marion, her older daughter who went to high school in town. She intended to start university in the fall. All of the schools were still closed for the summer, and her children mostly stayed at home, helping out with chores and preparing for the coming school year. Catherine did not hear her and, as well, she was not aware of the background eating and whispering noises at the table.

'Aren't you coming to eat with us?' yelled Richard, her husband. Her three children momentarily stopped eating and waited for a reply. She absentmindedly turned the tap off and delicately took the kitchen towel and flattened it out on the small table. She pleated it so that its sharp seams became invisible. She lifelessly moved over to the dining table and stared at them without taking notice of anyone in particular, for none of them could enlighten her.

'Are you going to stare us to death, Mom?' cried Keith, her younger son, who was nine years old and was still considered the baby of the family. He slammed his fork on his plate, and the sharp bang briefly chased away his mother's sorrow and anger. He started to hum the song, *Turning Time*:

The time is turning to light
Singing my fears away beyond the night
You can see how my life crying is to be
O community, loving community, you're the key in me
I'm thankful, so thankful to be with you
For you have been with me since my youth

All the leaves are changing
To shuffle away the past and weak from the living
The wind whistling it out to the trees
As the dark clouds and rain setting in to wash me free
I'm thankful, thankful to you for being with me
For my life shows me sharing is the way to be

All for love, and the love that makes me right
And without you, I couldn't have been upright
See my fisherman's life has no holes
I'm thankful, thankful for searching the ocean for my lost
soul
And I found the community to roam in
I'm so thankful for what my community has been
All singing out my name

And I won't be coming in vain
I sing farewell to you
For you've shown the community in me.

'Shut up! How could you make fun of everything?' she screamed
Keith down as well as everyone else at the table. Everyone was
surprised at her peculiar behavior.

'Aren't you eating?' insisted Richard, reaffirming his leadership
role in the house.

'No, I'm not hungry. Your grandpa cleaned up his whole apartment this morning.'

'Are you kidding? He asked me to do it this morning. At seven thirty just after Edwin took his breakfast down,' Marion said pleasantly. 'And you know what's more? I'll tell you. He was joyfully humming *Turning Time* this morning. He gave me a new bike if you want to know. It cost three hundred dollars. I'd say, I'm his favorite,' she said, giving Keith a big smile.

'That's not fair! She always gets something. How come he always gives you something? And me, nothing!' Keith jealously cried. 'And I always buy him his cigarettes, too. And he was singing that dumb song, too.'

'You never do anything for him! When he asks you to go to the store for him, you don't go. He has to pay you, first. I'm his favorite; I even look like Grandma. And my name is the same as Grandma,' she said with a smug smile.

'That's a lie! Grandma's name is Marina, not stupid Marion. That's not fair, Mom!' screamed Keith as he pushed his chair back angrily and left the table without finishing his dinner.

'Where do you think you're going?' Catherine asked seriously with a stern face, as he was about to open the inside door that went downstairs.

'You know, it isn't fair! Now, she has two bicycles, and me, I still have an old one,' he sadly grumbled with tears in his eyes.

'Will you hush up? You're crying like a little baby,' said Marion. Then confidentially she added, 'You can have my old one if you like.'

'All you guys ever do in this place is fight and quarrel and nothing else, protested Edwin. 'Grandpa gave me this, Grandpa didn't give me that. I went to town and bought the bike for him last week. All this time it has been in the garage. I took it out this morning for him.' He had the distance of one who knew the everyday living activities around the house. He was much more independent than his siblings. He spent a lot of time outside with friends and often got into a lot of trouble with his parents. He often came home late at night and ran away with the fishing boat on several occasions. And now words were floating around that he had made his girlfriend, Janet, pregnant.

Being only seventeen, just a year-and-a-half younger than his sister, he had adult-size problems.

'At five this morning, he started to hum that song like he'd won a million,' Edwin continued. 'It was dark and pouring by the gallon outside. At six o'clock, Grandpa got me to clean up the summer junk from the front lawn. In the heavy rain, he even went to the dock this morning. He told me that it was gonna be bright and sunny today. I should tell you all—I don't ask him for any handouts like you two morons. Always wanting to know how much you could get off him. And if I want to do something for him, I do it. If I don't, I don't. And that's all there is to it!'

Marion quickly wore an unsympathetic look: 'Don't give me your two-cent morality! Keep it for yourself! What are you going to do— quit school to support Janet for the rest of your life? Dad can take you on as a hand. Mom should have kicked you out of the house a long time ago. You see what you've done to her with all your stupid problems?'

'That's enough! It's going too far, now. Why don't you all just sit and eat like civilized human beings, for once,' Richard said calmly and firmly. He'd gotten up at ten o'clock that morning because it was Sunday. He realized that he hardly ever ate with his whole family together, and his children were growing too quickly for him.

'Why don't you tell Mom that, not us. Look how she's standing there and not saying a word to anyone. What is eating you up, Mom?' she wholeheartedly asked her daydreaming mother.

'All of you, you are a bunch of egoists. You only think about yourselves. People could just die, right in front of you! And none of you would care!' her uncontrollable grief ran over. She walked to the couch and sat in the middle with both hands covering her face to hide her sorrow and loneliness.

Her outburst surprised them; the children were looking at their father for an explanation, but he was completely bemused and thought that Edwin had done something awful again. Richard was furiously angry with him, his pupils widened, and his facial muscles reddened: 'You-u again!' quacked out from his grinning teeth, as he stopped short. Marion hated how both of them always argued and shouted at each other. She felt like running away from home, but she knew that she had to endure this until she started university. It was much more than their quarreling all the time; she would like to be free in a big city where nobody knew who she was and she could meet young men of her age. And her brother's girlfriend being pregnant worsened the cry of her own sexual self-identity. She abruptly left the table and went to her mother, sat at her side and exchanged roles. Catherine's hands still covered her face but didn't hide her pain; she collapsed into her daughter's arms. Marion held her mother tightly to protect her. She tried harder to pull her mother closer, but her mother's body was too cold to be warmed up. Marion passed her hand over her mother's hair while Catherine rested her face on her daughter's shoulder.

'I want a bike, too,' cried Keith, coming toward his mother and sitting at the other side of her. 'I'll never go to the store for him again. Let him send me, but I'm not going anymore, and that's final!'

Catharine hesitantly freed herself and wiped her running nose with her hand without removing it from her tormented stomach. She opened her emptied heart with both arms, extending them parallel to the couch, and then closed them in, tenderly, while bringing in her two children to her breast. She pulled them closer to her body as if keeping them alive and then murmured, 'Marion, go and get the doctor. Tell him to come over now.'

'What's the matter, mom? Are you sick or something?' she questioned, as her investigating eyes tried to detect physical symptoms.

'Don't ask anymore questions, just go, now,' she kindly requested. Marion got up and walked around a little in the living room. Everyone else was silent and could not understand Catherine's queer behavior. 'And you, Keith, go and tell your Aunt Betty to come now. At the same time, don't forget to tell Lewis to come over, too.' Lewis was Mr Cougar's best friend and fishing partner.

'Wait a minute! What's all this nonsense?' screamed Richard. 'What's the hell is going on around here?' But Catherine was not attentive to him.

'Go now, Keith.' And staring at her husband, 'Dad wants to see you right now,' she mumbled.

Richard shook his head in amazement, for he felt as though nobody was making sense, and his wife was giving orders and sending everyone to perform some sort of incomprehensible chores. Catherine waited for Keith to leave, but he hesitated near the outside door as though he would miss something. 'Please, Richard!' she begged. 'Go and see dad. It's really important.'

'Ok, if you put it that way, but he's to wait till I wash my hands,' he answered, suspicious, and thinking about killing some time by lingering in the kitchen in the hope that she would reveal her motive. But she only stared at him absent-mindedly.

'Alright, I'm going now,' cried Richard. He thought he knew his wife like the back of his own hand. He took a second look at her before he opened the inside door and, still faced with her silence, he unwillingly descended the stairs. Catherine stood up and began to clear the table as Keith and Marion waited by the outside door for some more encouragement. Tired of the tedious game, Marion finally took Keith by the hand and went out.

'Did you notice anything strange?' asked the Timeman.

'No, what do you mean?'

'Look attentively at Edwin's behavior.' The Timeman stopped time and then reversed it back to Catherine entering the door. Catherine, Richard, Marion, and Keith behaved exactly as before. Edwin was different. He stood up and walked to the window. He thought about today as being a unique day for some reason.

'Yes, he went to the window.... I perceived his thoughts. What's your point, Timeman?'

'His soul will be mine in the way I possess yours. I have to conquer him. And string him up in my realm of time.'

'Edwin, that's incredible. You defy all levels of consciousness. The Timeman's cell couldn't enslave a free mind,' Mr Cougar said, thinking that Edwin could hear him.

'Edwin can't help you. He belongs to me,' affirmed the Timeman. Mr Cougar reflected a little. He changed the subject because he didn't want the Timeman to see Edwin as a threat.

'Does my body have any experience of what I am observing now?' Mr Cougar asked.

'The interaction between your body and your higher level of consciousness is quite subtle. The lower level has to decode the answer after the flash is long gone. Now, you're helpless to interfere with reality. You would need the awareness of the lower level – the body to cause changes.'

'A useless metaphysical being, I am,' added Mr Cougar, 'thought without brain activities. And yet, I couldn't survive independently from my physical nature. You want me to give up the significance of my life, the community soul, creating friendship, and wanting to be remembered by others.'

'Community soul doesn't exist! Your last thought before death occupies a permanent place in the domain of time. That's the soul. Ralph, don't look so disappointed. Bear with me and you'll learn about the nature of your soul.'

'It is like the devil promising paradise to me.'

'How else could you abandon your naïve view of life, death, and the nature of the soul? I offer you the truth. Have you already forgotten Catherine's pain and suffering?'

'She is very realistic in her feelings. Nothing can change the fact that she's my daughter,' he said, thinking that the Timeman wouldn't push the matter any further.

'Yes, she is very sensitive and honest with her feelings. Wouldn't you say that Catherine is like *Lear's* daughter, Cornelia?'

'I don't know. But it is ridiculous to believe that my death causes real suffering. And if it does, my agony would be immeasurable.'

'Quite wordy, you are. What you see next would convince you of your ignorance. Your irrational beliefs of death and soul,' Mr Cougar observed a series of events before him.

12:30 Catherine's Flashes

'Are you Ok?' asked Edwin, wondering about his mother's absurd behavior of getting everyone around her to commit atrocities. 'You really know how to make people disappear. So, what's all this fuss about, sending everybody off to do some ridiculous chore?' His mother was still lost in her meaningless housework, almost withdrawn from the outside world, and entertaining images that she believed to be her ideal. And that they, in turn, had fashioned her self-identity.

'Do you remember,' she asked, 'when you were a little boy running on the shore? You liked us to chase you in the sand. Oh, I can remember how your little skinny feet could get the sand flying after you. All day long you wanted us to run after you. Whenever we took a break, you always threw a temper tantrum. You were very special in your own way and very carefree, too. You didn't want to make a sand castle, war tanks, and ships like the other kids. You wanted us to build a sand lake that could float in the water. You can't imagine how much fun I had on that sandy shore. It's like it was only yesterday.

'Oh yea, how your grandpa used to chase me on the shore, I tell you. He could never catch me. No matter what he did, I would slip away from him. I'd glide off the sand like a snake zigzagging. Oh, the warm sands under my feet. It felt like bathing in gold dust, the tiny grains tickling my feet. How I used to enjoy squeezing it between my toes. I used to cover my whole body with those powdered grains. I loved digging a huge hole in the sand, and then I'd slowly cover myself with the top layer of sand. For hours I used to sleep in that hole. Oh, God! I can still feel the sand tickling my body. You know, I wasn't into chasing and throwing rocks at sea gulls like the other kids. I listened to how the sand talked to my body, telling me funny stories about other kids and folks who had walked on the shore.

'One evening, the sun was just about to go down when your grandpa and me were fooling around on the shore. His sandy-blond hair radiated around his head. His entire body had turned golden. His face seemed to melt in the glow that was like a golden flame around him. Oh, how scary that was. How silly I was to think he'd melt away from me. People don't fly away. I was too young then, a little girl. But it really scared me like hell! I'll never forget how frightened I was.

'After school, I would run home quickly, change my clothes, and then run off to the harbor before he could leave. He had to take me with him, or else I'd stand there in that spot until he came back. He knew how stubborn I was, so he took me with them. Lewis would prepare a great snack for me, black cake with cookies and all. He somehow knew which day I was coming. But dad always told him to stop spoiling me. He never listened to dad, because he was much older. When dad wanted me to stay in the cabin, Lewis would have something for me to do on deck, like helping them set the net or control the rope. After a month, I was like a regular hand on the boat. I helped them with the net every Wednesday and Friday afternoon.

'When I was older like you, I was already working as a hired hand. I could do anything like a man. And dad didn't mind at all. Sometimes, he had to wait for me in the afternoon, because I had too much schoolwork to do. Then we were the last ones going out to set our nets. Some boats had to wait for us to finish, and then we'd all come in together. You see why I couldn't go off to school far away. I was barely able to finish high school. Some afternoons, when the ocean was calm, I spent most of my time doing homework in the cabin. But when it was rough, I had to help out and couldn't do schoolwork. I couldn't do school work in bad weather. Those were the days, being in the open ocean with waves splashing against the boat. In between chores I tried to enjoy the setting sun sinking on the horizon. The spectacular golden streams playing off the surface of the water couldn't do any of my homework. It couldn't keep the boat in position. All this I had to do out there. At least I was completely free. But now, the sun in my life will disappear forever.'

'Mom, you're talking to yourself! You're carrying the same plate in your hand around the kitchen. Are you Ok, or something?' As Edwin continued to make a salt hill with scattered grains from the bottle that he had accidentally tipped over on the table, her babbling mind continued, uninterrupted by loose remarks.

'I used to bring him home every Saturday evening when he went out drinking. Sometimes he was at a friend's place. And when he wasn't there, I could find him at Joe's Restaurant. Whenever dad's friends saw me coming, they said to him, "Look, your police are coming for you." Oh yes, those were the days. Instead of bringing him straight home, I used to sit around with them. But I had to make sure he didn't order any more alcohol. In the restaurant, everybody would want to stuff me up. Whatever I wanted, I could get. I was a little princess. A princess. Sometimes, they spoke about certain things, mostly nasty things about other people. They thought that I was too young to understand their conversation. But I wasn't. Though I was no more than six or seven years old when I started to drag him home...' She took a pause as she recollected the fight in the restaurant, and entertained it for a while.

Edwin held his head down while he listened to her, licking the sticky grains off his index finger, thinking about how in most places children could not walk alone. For it would be child neglect, and it would also be against the law for them to roam the streets after dark. Edwin finally arrived at what was bothering him all this time: *Is she going to die? Calling the doctor and sending everyone away except me. Only dying people talk about their childhood. But why is she telling me all this stuff? What is she up to? I hate suspense, being kept in the dark.* He tried to get her attention by licking his lips loudly, but she was arranging the cupboard as she unconsciously compared its order with her clothing. He realized it was useless to interrupt her, for he had enough of his own problems at hand. And the worst for him was her nagging and sobbing.

'Some men were arguing in the restaurant; then they started to fight. In less than a split second, everything was flying around like crazy—bottles, chairs, tables, and all. Everyone went crazy. I was so scared, so I hid under the table. When Dad realized I was there, he went crazy, fighting with everyone to protect his little princess. I had my eyes closed and I was terrified. I was so frightened that I didn't really know what was happening. I recall that the gun went off, and then everything was silent. Joe always had it under the counter. He had only blown off the front window. Thank God nobody got hurt. Finally, dad got me out from under the table. Oh, I was crying like a little hairless monkey. Nobody could get me loose from him. He took me home just like that. My arms were wrapped around his neck, and my little skinny legs clamped around his stomach. Just like a lobster grabbing itself onto a finger.

'When we got home, Dad told me not to tell Mom. But I was crying non-stop, and she could barely free me from dad. He had to tell her. I can't recall how they separated us. For sure because of that, Mom and Dad didn't speak to each other for days. Dad blamed Mom for sending me. And Mom blamed Dad for almost getting me killed because of his Saturday night drinking with friends. Oh, that was something.

'At first, Mom and I used to go out in the evening and look for Dad. We would look all over the place. Sometimes we couldn't find him. If he was at Joe's, Mom would stay outside while I went in and got him. Sometimes she went home without us. Like that, Mom started to send me out to get him. She didn't want to be among those drunken men, and it would really look bad for a woman to go in. Mom always wanted Betty to come with me, but she was different. She only cared about reading and playing her flute when she wasn't chasing boys. As of today, she's still playing it.' Catherine briefly realized herself and then glanced at her son. He was still playing with the salt, but she could not really see such details other than thinking how much Edwin resembled his grandfather.

'You like fishing? Don't you?' She moved closer to him and picked up the remaining salt on the table. He was slightly frightened to answer her sudden question.

'Yea! Why ask?'

'It's hard to tell. You don't say anything much, these days.'

'What there's to say? Nothing.'

'Do you want to quit school and help your dad out?'

'No. I don't have to quit school to help out dad. To be out of here is the only safe place for me. Nobody to jump at me every five minutes. To drive me crazy!'

'I did both—working and studying—until I finished high school. If you really want something, you can get it.'

'So, what's your lecture about today? I've already done drugs, stayed out late, missed classes, had poor grades, gotten Janet pregnant, and heaven knows what. I was getting suspicious at first; I thought you were going to kick the bucket. But I should have known, shouldn't I? I know your type by now. Don't worry. I'll still do the opposite of what you say.' He was ready for the big lecture that he expected would come.

'No, Edwin! You've got me wrong. I tried very hard to bring you up straight and decent. The harder I tried, the worst it got. You just revolted against everything. I always tried so hard to be your best friend and a mother at the same time, but we got further and further apart for some reason. It really hurts me. Your ways ripped my guts up with a dull knife. You don't know how much it hurts me when I see my loved one going the wrong way. No mother wants her children to suffer, to take drugs, to go down the drain. And then end up in jail. You want me to be calm and rational. If this is what you expect from us, you don't need parents; you need a robot.'

She came over and sat in front of him blowing her wet nose and wiping her irritated eyes. 'You don't even know anything!' She groaned, and wiped her eyes some more. How could she tell him what was on her mind? She thought that perhaps he was too childish to understand death. He should have known his grandfather better than anyone else. At least, better than her.

He sat there and rarely looked at her. He felt helpless for not showing the right sentiment at this moment. He did not know what to feel, for he was most confused. 'You're hiding your true feelings of guilt and bad conscience because you denied me parental love. So, you think that I sought closeness, tenderness, and warmth from Janet. You don't see me as a tragic hero. And you should mostly blame yourself for my waywardness.'

Though Edwin spent a lot of his time with his grandfather, everyone else thought he was performing mischievous and delinquent acts with his friends. Whenever he stayed out at night, he slept at his grandfather's apartment. After his grandmother died, he used to take long walks during the night with his grandfather, going to the beach and the dock, looking at the stars, and listening to the splashing and rolling waves. His grandfather was his mentor. He taught him to walk with his feet and not with his mouth, to feel with his body and not his mind. Unfortunately, his mother did not really hear him.

'What did he really tell you this morning?' she interrogated.

'Who?'

'Your grandpa!'

'I already said it. Not much.'

'Not only to clean up the yard around the house.'

'I don't get you! What's all this crap about?'

'Edwin! Will you be on the level with me for once?'

'I told you this before. I think he went down to the dock. About five this morning. Taking his usual morning stroll, I guess. Whenever the tide is at its prime and deposits its daily treasures, he goes out. Oh, yes! If you could have seen it—he was very happy. He was humming something like, "What a man can do on a day like this." Then he told me to pick up the yard on a marvelous day like this. I think he said something like, "This year will be a wonderful year for fishing".' Edwin was suspicious of his mother who stared at him for some more news.

Why did she send for the doctor and Aunt Betty? he thought, as he took a quick glance at her.

'So, that's it? He didn't say anything more?'

'What's this the inquisition? You never ask me any of these stupid questions before. You only order us around! The only time people call the doctor for a house visit is when they're having babies. You're

getting a committee to discuss my future with Janet, aren't you? And
if things don't work out with an abortion, you'll send Dad to talk to
Grandpa about sharing his apartment. Oh, you really plan everything
for me! You didn't leave anything out!' He stood up abruptly but still
didn't leave. It would be more interesting to find out how much others
knew about his situation. For Janet had unintentionally revealed her
pregnancy without revealing who the father was; but everyone quickly
put one and one together. Until now, he had never been directly
confronted as to whether he was the father, and he had no inclination
to change attitudes about him.

'No, Edwin! It's your grandpa,' she said angrily and then banged
the table heavily with both hands. The bang echoed in the house,
giving Edwin a shock like a lightning bolt and making him very scared.
The vibration in the floor under his feet told him that she had gone
beyond her limit.

She's getting out of control, he thought, as his enlarged eyes
showed fear. He was still preparing himself for some sort of physical
aggression; with red cheeks, he scanned her for any loose clues, and
he was ready in case he had to make a quick escape.

'Sorry, for frightening you.' Catherine was feeling frustrated about
herself, her inability to be straight about her father's ultimatum. Her
apology rapidly reduced her son's tension. 'You wouldn't say very
much if I went to town at four today and never return, would you?'

He looked at her and raised both shoulders. 'I don't know.'

'If I had to go to the hospital, it'd bother you, wouldn't it?'

'Will you quit this cat and mouse game! So, you have to go to the
hospital, I get it. For what? And how long?' Suddenly he was thinking
it had to be something very important. Perhaps, she had cancer. He
started to feel sorry. His hands were wet and his face turned pale.
He felt completely lost, for he believed that he was not the right
person for her to confide in.

'Come on, Mom! Everything's gonna be all right! You don't have
to worry about a thing.'

'Sorry Edwin, it's not me.' She hesitated for a while. 'It's worse
than if I had to die. Wait till your father is here, he'll tell you. Oh God,

am I going crazy?' She started to cry again, for she could not overcome her identity with her childhood and her pain.

'Ok, if you say so.' He went to the fridge. 'Would you like something to drink?'

'Yes, please. Plain water will do.'

Catherine's revelation of her past absorbed her father. He clearly remembered the little incident in the bar. 'She idealizes me. Her emotions are noble. But that's the wrong way to approach life. What I meant to her should be the community way of life, the principle of life – the soul. She should try to cultivate as many friends as possible. And that counts the most in life. Like this - fraternity, liberty, equality, and respect would grow in her. The principle of the community soul is about how to live with others. In a community, everybody helps to mold each other. And this is a way to retain self-integrity.'

'Ralph, she knows that you won't die. You didn't show her any sign of dying. She's pragmatic. She measures life with her community's reaction, embarrassment. Obviously, you don't truly understand how she feels about you.'

'I don't know her mind as well as you do. She has brought so much joy into my life. And her love alone will keep me alive eternally. Please show me some other events because I can't express much sentiment in your presence,' Mr Cougar said. The Timeman allowed time to flow around these events without any interruption.

12:45 The First Assembly

Stairs screeching with heavy and steady footsteps became louder.
Catherine and Edwin's ears closely counted the primitive beats. The
sound halted near the closed inner door as though he took a precaution
against the unexpected leaping out from a hidden corner. He hesitated
for the final breath to mount his courage and undertake the last
confrontation, and was indecisive about the emotional strain his news
would have for Catherine. Richard opened it slowly, exposing his
pale face. They were at the table, and he walked straight to them.
While he wished that each step would take him backwards, he rubbed
his hands and prepared his mouth to say something. His vocal chords
did not heed his command. He cleared his throat in desperation, but
nothing noticeable came out. Then suddenly, like a hurricane:
'Somebody is going haywire around here!' he growled like a wild
animal, 'And it's not me!' The experience downstairs was utterly
incomprehensible: a strong and healthy person talking about his coming
death. He shook his head in disbelief as he stared at the long dread-
filled faces looking at him while he tried to get some control over
himself. 'What's the hell going around here?' he asked again, and he
waited for someone to enlighten him.

'Go and close the door, Edwin,' cried Catherine, wanting Richard
to calm down a little, for she now felt a bit of relief. She was not the
only one who held the secret. Appearing to be rational over her
situation when the other partner was down, 'Edwin, get your dad
something to drink.'

'He asked me to help him move to the living room. I had to move
his bed, too! When I was moving his bed, he went to the kitchen and

poured himself a full glass of apple juice and grabbed a handful of cookies. Then he smiled at me. And said, "You've to be strong and fit with a clean head." And then he brushed his teeth and went to lie in his bed. That's not all! I had to put his bed's head up, in a comfortable sitting position like a maharaja. He said to me, "Today, I expect a lot of visitors".'

'Here, Dad.' Edwin gave him a glass of juice. Richard took a sip without showing any sign of wanting to sit, and then he paced the room.

Edwin returned to his regular place. 'Does he think we're crazy or something? Has he lost his bearings? Nobody in his right mind would say, "My dear Richard! It's so wonderful to express my deepest gratitude and goodbye to you". The next moment, he jumped out of his bed like a fox and embraced me forcefully. And then like the other side of a coin, he gently and tenderly wept all over me—worse than a child. Here comes his golden line: "I'm going to die today at four o'clock!" For crying out loud! Yes, he said he wanted to be comfortable and ready for it among his friends who would still be in a state of disbelief because dying should not be something to joke about, especially with others' feelings.'

'At four, he said?' Edwin impatiently cried, showing a bit of concern, for he should have anticipated something unusual from his grandpa's strange behavior.

'Don't you hear so good anymore? Yes, four! He looks as if he hasn't shaved and cut his hair for years. You should see how much older he looks. Everything is strange,' he replied with some relief as he passed the responsibility down the line, reducing its intense effects.

'So, it's today,' Edwin murmured, 'It must be the cycle! Wholly meatball! The terror of the sea and the terror under the sea meet!' He quickly pushed his chair away and skipped stairs to reach downstairs.

'What did you say?' yelled Catherine, for he had no time to turn back and answer her. Richard appeared to unravel some mental knots as he sat near his wife. They embraced each other. He was trying to uplift her because this was her father they were discussing.

'What are we going to do?' asked Richard, for the mourning had already started.

'I don't know,' she murmured. 'He isn't sick. If he were, I'd understand, but he isn't, Richard.' He tried to comfort his wife, but she was trembling with fear and uncertainty.

'He's your father, dear.'

'Honestly,' she whispered. 'I don't know. To tell you the truth, if I had to choose between you and Dad, I could.... Now, our whole lives, everything we've worked for, is crumbling. Our entire family will have to live in shame and disgrace. We won't be able to lift our heads in the street.'

'No dear, there isn't any shame, everything's gonna be OK,' he comforted.

'He isn't going to die. Wait and see! It'd be unbearable for our children. What's next? We'd have to move away from here. Everyone knows us. O, Richard, can't you see? I don't know what to do.'

'It's Ok. He's absolutely certain, dear. He means it, too. I was astonished and shocked when he said it. But something in his voice and eyes told me he meant it, dear. He said we could keep the house and fishing boat, if that'd make you feel any better!' She pulled herself away from him with contempt. 'Yes, he gives the boat to Edwin.'

'How can you say such nonsense? Don't you have any feelings? For sure you want him to die. How can you think about money? Oh, God! What am I saying? Sorry, dear! I know you don't mean it,' she switched her mood abruptly. 'It's the shock, so much death around here, in such a short time. It's driving everybody insane.'

'I'm sorry dear,' apologizing for his insensitive remark, 'I just want to tell you he's all prepared to go. That's all.'

The doorbell rang. Both Keith and Marion entered first to warn their parents about the visitor coming with them; Dr Robinson slowly followed them. He was an all-rounder. He looked much older than his late sixties, was too chubby for his height, had gray hair covering his ears, and held a brown medical bag in his hand. He waited near the door, as he tried to regain his breath. Both Richard and Catherine went to the door and greeted him. 'I'm so pleased you could come over so quickly,' she said in a mournful voice that drew the doctor's attention to her reddish eyes.

'Hi Doc!' cried Richard.

'Hello Richard! Don't tell me you're into wife-battering?' he greeted back with an over-bearing voice that showed his affirmative and self-assured personality.

'You're not doing so badly yourself,' replied Richard.

'It's really nothing to see old friends, and it's the best way to burn extra calories,' he moved his belly up and down with his hand while his face lit up with a friendly smile.

'Would you like something to drink?' asked Catherine, leading the way toward the living room.

'Since you ask, and if you don't really mind, a glass of white wine will do. I haven't had the chance to take my appetizer yet. Marion busted in and dragged me away from the table without showing any respect for a good meal.'

Marion got the wine while both Catherine and the doctor sat on the couch with Richard in the armchair and Keith standing around.

'How is fishing these days?' the doctor asked, being naturally comfortable and lightheaded but not nosy.

'Well, the nets are old and need some repairing. Other than that, I can't complain. It's been a good season so far,' replied Richard. He wanted someone else to take over the conversation.

'Doc, guess what?' Keith asked enthusiastically.

'Let me see, you burnt the school building down.'

'Are you crazy? Dad would kill me if I did that!'

'What then?'

'Aunt Betty is coming over, too.' Keith had met her in the street while she was going to a friend's place.

'Really. So how is school young man?'

'You should know it. We're on holiday.' The doctor agreed with him, and Richard glanced at his wife as a sign to get to the point.

'Well Doc, it's not us. It's Dad,' Catherine nervously cried, and uncontrollable tears began to roll off her cheek.

'He said he's going to die today,' Richard added quickly.

'Come on! Richard, don't be so hard on yourself. There's no need to have a crisis,' said the doctor, grinning insensitively; and yet, he had a strong sense of self-assurance about his patient would recover amazingly. Marion returned with a glass of wine and handed it to the doctor.

'Thanks. You really know how to keep an old man smiling,' and his pupils enlarged while he licked his lips. Marion went to comfort her mother, but she joined her in weeping instead.

'It's good for him! Let him die. He didn't want to get me a bike,' cried Keith. For the notion of death had not penetrated his playfulness. He could not sensationalize sorrow, grief, loss, emotional suffering, and death. Appearing not to have a profound thought about losing a loved one, other children of his age would wallow on the floor to show that their suffering was bigger than anyone else's.

'Maybe, he had a slight fever, and it's giving him some delirium. This always happens with older couples, especially when the wife dies first. The husband becomes very lonely and depressed. He wants to die, too. Ralph wants to jump onto the same bandwagon as Marina. Don't worry about anything. He's just saying how he feels. This first six-month period is very hard for him. I assure you that you don't have anything to worry about. He's going through a mild crisis because he doesn't have his Marina around anymore. It's hard you know. So, Catherine, calm down. There's nothing to worry about. In a jiffy, he'll forget everything, this nonsense of dying.' Cheerful things often flew off him, and he could not easily shift to the negative side of life.

The doorbell rang again; Keith ran to open it. 'Aunt Betty is here,' he shouted for everyone to hear. She wore a jacket and skirt like an arrogant businesswoman practicing lynching at school. The black handbag that hung on her shoulder matched her shoes, and dress evoked a terrifying image of her working overtime in dark alleys. Except for her over use of cosmetics and perfume to overcome Sandreef's fishy smell, her short hair agreed with any season. She was quite charming and a born optimist, which made her adaptable to any situations. Carrying such an aroma made her likable.

'You never whipped out the answer to me like that at school,' Betty cried.

'How could I? You already knew all the answers before you asked us questions. It killed the fun in getting them,' answered Keith.

'Hello, where is everyone hiding?' she joyfully asked without considering herself a guest. 'Is this how Catherine treated her dignified guest: her indignant sister?'

'In the living room, Aunt Betty. Doctor Robinson is here, too,' answered Keith, and he felt so pleased to be helpful.

'Thanks,' she marched toward them without showing any sign of surprise. 'Hello, you big oaf!' Betty greeted Richard, as she glanced over to the doctor who stood up. 'Look at yourself, doc!' She exchanged a strong handshake with the doctor. 'You should really see a doctor. You're getting too fat and gray.'

'Betty, you'll never change. Are you still bending straight kids at school?'

'They need a brain surgeon nowadays, not a teacher.' First, she said hello to Marion who took a chair near her father, and then she said hello to Catherine. 'And how is my little baby sister doing these days? Don't say you're having another babe!' She looked at her belly and then sat between Catherine and the doctor. In the next moment, she started to rub Catherine's belly, and Catherine quickly pushed Betty's hand away. 'Oh, it looks like Richard is shooting blanks. Could it be you're eating everyone else's food around here,' she giggled and gave her sister a friendly clap on her leg. This only made Catherine angrier.

'No, Betty. Can't you ever be serious for once? You're so nosy and pushy,' Catherine complained.

'You mean I'm happy and cheerful even if the world is crumbling under Catherine's feet? Sorry dear, you take everything too seriously,' she continued jokingly, and then she gave the doctor a strong punch that nearly knocked over his wine glass. 'The only time this gray fox makes house visits is to pull out an uncooked bun from the oven!' Smiling at the doctor, she put her arm on his shoulder.

'I think I'll take another glass. It's a really good appetizer. You should try some, Betty,' said the doctor, giving Marion the hint to fetch some.

'For Catherine's taste, nobody needs a witch doctor around,' cried Betty who took the doctor's empty glass and sniffed it. 'Catherine knows more about nail removers than vinegar. Look at Richard! He looks worst than a sour lemon. I bet this vinegar kills out all the friendly germs in his mouth.' Richard knew that Betty was not the person to invite on any occasions, but she had to be here. 'So, where is the big show today? Inviting me here surely takes away all your joy. Doesn't it?'

Betty eyed Marion refilling the doctor's glass; as she was handing it to him, Betty intercepted and took a sip from it. 'This is flatter than a flounder! Anyway, get me a glass, Marion, my angel. You can't allow this gray fox to be a lonely drunkard,' she grinned and made everyone else almost frustrated.

'Grandpa is going to kick the bucket today! That teaches him a good lesson. He didn't want to buy me a bicycle,' interrupted Keith, being very obsessive and childish about a new bike.

Catherine stared at him. 'Will you hush up?'

'So, he wants to kick the bucket, eh!' Betty said. 'Is that how he tells me to pay up? I hope he's already taken care of his bills, too. It's really funny,' she smiled, 'Kicking the bucket crap. Hey, gray fox, they don't need you here, a priest. Yeah, Keith! Go and get the soul-man to polish him up.'

'It's true, Betty,' Catherine interrupted her sister and painfully murmured. 'He said he'd die at four today.'

'Oh, you're always too sensitive! Why not at five?' she started to laugh a bit too loudly as she checked her watch. 'Go and change the clock in his room. Even better yet, take the battery out. He wouldn't know today from tomorrow. If the old buzzer wants to buzz off, it's the right time to open a bottle. If I'd known earlier, I'd have told everyone to come over for a good laugh. Keith, go and get them for me. And tell them to bring over a good bottle of wine,' smiling at him with approval. He glanced at his mother for permission, but she only stared at Richard in an attempt to be rescued from her offensive sister; but he wanted to stay out of the family's dispute. 'Why don't we go downstairs and see him before he croaks!' Betty continued.

'He's only three hours and thirty-eight minutes away from his grave.'
Everyone felt sympathetic at her suggestion. 'Not you, Keith! You've
work to do, remember? Catherine, where's your Romeo? I've not
seen him yet.'

'Edwin is downstairs with his grandpa,' replied Richard.'

'So, I see; the old goat already gets you to believe in absurdities.
Doc, are you ready to commit atrocities?'

'Not really. Let's go and see the patient.' The doctor showed
some difficulties standing up because the couch was much lower
than his own. Since Richard was closer to the door, he led the way,
followed by the doctor, Betty, and Marion. As Catherine tailed along
slowly, she told Keith to tell some neighbors to come over, too.

'Oh, no! Wait a minute,' Keith objected, 'if Marion doesn't lend
me her new bike, I'm not going.'

'Ok, take it!' cried Catherine, answering for Marion who would
also have tried to get rid of him for a while.

'Hum, a new bike, twenty-one speeds, it must be like lightning,'
he joyfully sang, as he left by the outside stairs.

'Ralph, your daughters have unquestionable love for you. Where
is your gratitude? And what do you know about death? There are
many beliefs about the afterlife, but no evidence. Are you going to
heaven or hell? Do you also believe in reincarnation? The mystery of
death is for the living to unfold. Wouldn't you say so? Death—nothing
escapes me. Paradise, I offer everyone.'

'At least, you're very reassuring. How does the soul manifest
itself in your arena of time?'

'The last image or thought of a dying person I preserve eternally.
And he'll experience that thought or image forever in one of my time
cells.'

'My daughters love me. And we believe in community soul, and
friendships—all this is beyond a single person. And they can't be
strung up in your time cell.'

'Ralph, your thoughts are transparent to me. You want me to
forget Edwin. Because you think that he is innocent. You can't deceive
me.'

'Why don't you leave him out of this? He hasn't done anything against you. You want to enslave me in your time cell, not him.'

'He'll resist me in the future. And his nature is very unpredictable. My nature, Edwin has to worship, not your bloated community soul.'

'Does that mean you'll separate his mind from his body like what you have done to me? Although it is incomprehensible that you are interested in a harmless lad.'

'Any real threat to my reality will be strung up in one of my time cells. I can't slice his consciousness up because his levels of consciousness are too interconnected. But I'll take him whole. And he'll be powerless to interfere with reality.'

'You judge him too harshly.' Mr Cougar tried to change the subject: 'My sunshine will overcome your nature of death, if we fail.'

'Betty, she doesn't have any reflection on a high day. She makes shallow people like herself shine around her. Have you forgotten that Edwin went to see that lump lying in bed? It told him I was the most horrible creature. And I had only one desire—to consume everything in my path. Look at Edwin and how he is hurrying toward the ocean for help.

'Now, look closely. Each step towards his goal is a step away from his body.' Suddenly, Edwin folded on the shore in a sitting position as though he was contemplating the ocean and becoming unaware of his surrounding.

'Edwin, I'm the Timeman. Your grandpa has spoken about me. I've separated you from your body.'

'Edwin,' interrupted Mr Cougar.

'Grandpa! Where are you? I can hear your voice. Now I see you. But you look very different.' Edwin was scared out of his wits.

'The Timeman wants to show us his nature. We are communicating with our minds. Our bodies are only imaginary, not real. We can perceive the world around us without being able to alter anything. We are like prisoners in a time cell. We are trapped in the future while we see the present.'

'How can that be? It isn't possible. And who is the Timeman anyway? He can't do this to us,' he spoke rapidly.

AMO SULAIMAN

'Ralph, didn't you tell him about your doom?' the Timeman asked.

'So, you're the Timeman. I can't see you. And what doom are you talking about?'

'You're a treat to his destiny. He wants to know you much better because you can elude him. Just be yourself, Edwin...'

'A treat. I think he is mad!' said Edwin. 'There are supposed to be three of us here. For some reason, I have the impression that someone else is looking at us.'

'Quite remarkable,' answered the Timeman in his usual deep dry voice. 'I've all the reasons to have you with us.'

'All this is strange. A moment ago, I was walking along on the shore, I felt as though I was fainting. My feet gave away. At a glimpse I saw an endless chain before me. Some of its eyes were illuminated brightly. Some dim. And others were completely black. What's the meaning of all this?'

'Each chain's eye is a time cell. And a soul is a prisoner inside it,' answered the Timeman.

'I get it. My grandpa and I want to free those souls. And you don't want us to.'

'Edwin, we're like ghosts here. And the Timeman is a master of deception,' interrupted Mr Cougar.

'Deception, what do you know about it? Your meaningless babbling about the soul and death as being knowable should condemn you to my eternal time cell. Community soul is a fictitious entity. You, Edwin. You're supposed to help your grandpa to defend his community soul?'

'I would do anything to save my grandpa from you,' said Edwin, feeling sure about himself.

'And if you fail, I'll possess both of you like a curse. But if you succeed, I'll grand you one wish.'

'Don't worry, I won't fail. My grandpa has confidence in me. The community soul is my heart. And nobody can take away what is the closest to my heart,' he finished, hoping that his grandpa would assist him. But Mr Cougar thought that if he interrupted Edwin's spontaneity, he would fail and become the Timeman's prisoners.

'Before I allow you to observe the madness your grandpa has evoked, answer me truthfully. Has there been a rational argument for death? Don't tell me it's a natural process.'

'Grandpa,' said Edwin, urging him to say something.

And he did. 'Until now, psychology, religion, and biology haven't removed our inherited fear of death. But you are trying to tell me that I welcome it. And that I'm a fool. Death, we accept for its own sake, but not as a means for something else. Death appears as horrible and cruel for us; we don't want it to appear in any form in our minds. It's a forbidden domain for us. But if we do entertain it in our discussion, we try to elucidate death by introducing other abstract concepts— soul, eternal life, heaven, hell, and reincarnation. We do this because we want to reduce the mystery of death.

'Perhaps, you think that I also want to reduce some misunderstandings about death. And community soul has just done that. Let me reassure you one thing: community soul is about living. When a person lives by the principle of the soul, his good deeds continue long after that person has passed away. It doesn't matter how you regard me. Community soul enhances positive human values to live by.'

'Haven't you forgotten one thing?' asked the Timeman. 'You can't die. There isn't any escape for you. I ordain your destiny. Can't you see that I am real? Time is real. And it exists in all conceivable domains. Death, soul, and immortality obey the law of time. If time doesn't exist, perhaps you could speak about the existence of the soul in a meaningful way. I'm here to remove you fallacious judgments.'

'Don't listen to him, Grandpa! Your soul will exist as long as we remember you. And our view of the principle of the soul is quite pragmatic. Because we would like to be remembered after life. And we will do most anything for our souls.'

'You are more stubborn than I thought. Ralph, you can't die! Be my privileged guest and witness your slim and lean personality. With your premature announcement of death, I haven't seen any community soul yet. If you fail to demonstrate otherwise, you'll be abolished in my time cells.'

'Edwin, just be yourself,' cried Mr Cougar, as they found themselves involved in a set of new scenes.

13:00 Spreading the News

The new glittering blue bicycle leaned against the wall next to the outside stairs; it was obviously unlocked; sometimes people forgot to lock their house door before they went to bed; most people left their cars unlocked. Bicycles in the street were hardly ever chained, for the implicit norm suggested that there was no need to lock anything. Stealing and vandalism had no place in this small community; private properties were like the inhabitants here—people knew each other. Trust and honesty were allowed to grow eloquent roots in which material things underwent changes. Though some residents preferred to live in town and to keep a fair distance from others who had a similar philosophy: be a stranger to others and more so to oneself, very few inhabitants moved to town from Sandreef.

Keith took a few steps backwards and admired the bike as though the whole view had to be experienced like phenomenology—imagining himself flying over holes and bumps. He finally touched it and was impressed about twenty-one speeds. He wanted to use all the gears from the lowest to the highest. He sat on the soft saddle and rode; the cycle's brake handles slightly touched his father's car on the driveway. But he continued to peddle out of the yard. Luckily there was no front gate, because within that short distance from the house, he tried to switch several gears successively.

Now his bitter jealousy and new joy were fused together, making him more reckless and dangerous. He had the chance to squeeze out the maximum benefit from Marion's bicycle and to rub off all its authentic qualities so it could be reduced to a repulsive object. He quickly stopped and controlled the left handle; it was OK: 'That stupid crow and seagull could make anybody have an accident. Why do they have to make so much noise around here?' he said out loud, looking at both birds flying around the house then setting down on the roof.

He sped into the main road, using the two-wheeler like a deadly weapon to scar off coming cars and motorists. The self-reflection of his own well-being and safety rhymed with his community's history: nothing spectacular ever happened around here, not even a smashing accident. He knew that he was going to Buddy's house first, his cousin, who lived several streets away. For this short distance, he was obviously taking the longest way. The red stoplights did not mean a complete halt for him; he quickly made a right turn at the cross section and then quickly made another right into the main road. This trick was well known in big cities where people avoided stationary objects (like stagnant events) in their lives.

Arriving at his aunt's place, he stopped in the driveway and called. He rode several times into the garage's zinc door while he shouted for Buddy. Some neighbors heard his yelling and banging on the garage door. The opposite one was angry with him. 'What's the problem with you, Keith?' shouted Mrs Brown, who was in her glorious forties and had the sense to sniff out ingredients for her gossip pot.

'Grandpa is dying at four today!' he replied loud enough for the entire street to hear. He was very proud to deliver such news. Though she was shocked a bit, she waited for some more information to quench her craving mind.

'You little rascal!' screamed Buddy from the upstairs window, 'You want to break the door down?'

'Yea! How do you like this?' he asked, while getting off the cycle for Buddy to have a better view of it.

'That's for girls,' he answered, making Keith very angry and embarrassed.

'Whom do you think this is for!' holding his crotch out so Buddy could see the bulge between both hands. Being a slightly overweight and not having a girl friend yet, Buddy blushed and then pretended not to see Mrs Brown who was still surveying the scene.

'How vulgar!' she shouted, 'wait and see, I'll tell your mother. Your pants are getting too big for you.' Keeping her promise was one thing, but she often whipped a story up to make it the most interesting one there was.

'Stupid mutt!' Keith mumbled, but dared not say it loud.

'Yes, Mrs Brown. These young kids. They don't have any respect these days,' he said, smiling at Keith who was really in more trouble than he had asked for.

Feeling remorseful and lowering his head as a sign of defeat, Keith reported his news. 'Everybody should come over now, all of you. Grandpa is dying....' Mrs Brown and some other neighbors quickly closed their windows.

'You're pulling my leg.' cried Buddy.

'Ask your mom. She's there,' realizing that his dad would ground his pocket piece for a week whenever he heard a complaint involving him. He drifted further away from the content of his message; he noticed that Buddy had left the window open and then disappeared into the house. He jumped on his bike and rode off to the next street, showing how quickly he could overcome personal problems.

On the next street, in front of the Bergers' house, he called out for Mr Berger. 'Mr Berger, are you home? Is anybody home? Mr Berger!'

A senior citizen with a beard opened his front door, exposing his lunch in his mouth and babbled out politely, 'What is it?'

'Guess what? Grandpa....'

'Are you sure? Do you know what you're saying, lad?'

'Yes, sir. You can even ask Aunt Betty if you don't believe me.' This strong evidence sent him slightly staggering, and Keith could not understand how Mr Berger could stand so stupidly without saying anything.

'You meant, Ralph...my partner. This can't be!'

'Oh, yeah! Everybody is already there.'

Struggling for some breath, Mr Berger said, 'Ok, Keith, I'm coming over right away. Tell your grandpa to wait for me.' He vanished into the house without noticing Keith's new wheels. Keith was offended a bit, but he did not really mind because Mr Berger was too old to notice such details.

He rode from one street to the next, telling every passerby about today, and going to the last few remaining streets. Unfortunately, most residents had already gotten the message; he had a stern disappointment on his face, because he could not overwork the new toy. He decided to go to the schoolyard, which was at the other end of Sandreef where the main road ran straight to Rose Hall. He hoped to meet some friends there riding around the schoolhouse.

On his way, Mr and Mrs Foster, two retired citizens, stopped him. 'Tell me, Keith! We heard it from the radio that your grandpa is dying today at four o'clock. And they said that all his friends and neighbors should come over to say goodbye. Is that so? We want to give our condolences, too,' cried Mr Foster. Newspapers, radio stations, and TV companies paid about one hundred dollars for the best scoop of the week. And a contestant could be automatically qualified for the best one of the month for one thousand dollars. And the best of the year would bring five thousand dollars.

'Is it true? You bet your last buck, sir? If my grandpa says he'll kick the bucket, you can bet your life on it—he'll do it.'

'I see,' replied Mr Foster who was taken in by Keith's frankness.

'Oh, yes, you should know that everybody is coming over. I must hurry before I miss all this action.' He sped off quickly.

'Thank you, Keith. What a nice boy, he is,' declared Mrs Foster.

'Edwin,' the Timeman cried, 'your brother has shown no sentiment toward his grandpa's coming death.'

'Yes, he knows that Grandpa could die. But he shows no fear of death. You could only find this in some innocent people. Not only ignorant ones.'

'But there'll be no death in Sandreef,' the Timeman forcefully asserted.

'Timeman, you've missed the point again. Keith has just awakened the community. The life of my grandpa's soul will prevail over the shadow of any afterlife. You've seen some people of our community who are very receptive to my grandpa's call. Keith is stirring everyone to be ready for my grandpa's soul'

'That's the spirit of the community soul,' interrupted Mr Cougar. 'People are coming over for their own sake. Nothing materialistic brings them together, but only friendship. They realize that we share the best of ourselves together. And this holds friends and neighbors together. Had any of them been in my place, he would have been satisfied with his way of life, too. I trust my friends who are like myself. And my spirit will shine after my death.' The Timeman didn't make any comment. And Mr Cougar hoped that Edwin might learn not to challenge the Timeman directly. Edwin was wondering about why his grandpa was so calm and formal.

'If you think that the madness is finished, you're wrong. Let's see what else will happen,' the Timeman suggested and they followed and watched carefully.

13:15 Talking about Death

Speeding towards the school, thinking of meeting his friends there and hoping to have a race with them, Keith noticed his classmates Doug and Murray with their two-wheelers. They were riding around the schoolhouse slowly. He rode just next to them and stopped, 'How do you like my new baby?' asked Keith.

Doug looked at it very sarcastically, 'Wow, it's cool.' 'The only problem is that it isn't for you.' He searched for a reaction in Keith of depression or sorrow.

'Tell us Keith,' said Murray, hesitating about what he wanted to say because he knew very well he did not want Keith to throw a temper tantrum at him now. 'Is your grandpa really...going to...you know what?'

'Oh, yeah! Dead as a stone, I'd say!'

'Wow, that's cool!' cried Doug. 'That's the way. You dig it.' He passed his hand over Keith's bike and played with the gears. 'This stuff is neat. Isn't it for girls?' He knew that Keith was not a sissy, but riding a girl's bicycle still raised some doubts in his mind.

'It's Marion's...'

'Can we go and check your grandpa out, Keith?' asked Murray; he had observed a lot people going to the Cougar's. And his grandparents had died before he was born, so he had missed out from the thrills and spectacles of dying. And yet, the fear of it all was unimaginable.

'Timeman, wait a second,' interrupted Edwin, 'Murray believes what adults say. He also believes that if he looked at a dying person's face, he would get all the evidence of dying. Like this, he thinks that he would see death coming. And death for him isn't an abstract concept. But there are signs for it.'

'If you're finished, we can continued,' replied the Timeman.

'He's gonna flick off today. I wonder if his eyes will be open like a dead fish. That granny who used to live near us died at home. Her eyes were like an owl. That wasn't cool, man! They couldn't close them, so they had to get the doctor to stitch them closed. You should have seen them. Boy, you'd have dropped dead with fear. That was something,' cried Doug, trying to profoundly sensationalize his experience because the other two boys had not witnessed it.

'Yes, some people have a pleasant death,' Edwin interjected. Others, like the most horrible. Doug is like a young philosopher. He is asking how a person should die? Is there a good death or a bad one? He sees that death is a dreadful experience. This fear is darker than the blackest soul. And he thinks about when he will die. If he looks like the granny, death has to be very scary. This horror he had seen from the granny's face.' The Timeman allowed the events to continue.

'Come on, Doug! Keith wouldn't know that,' interrupted Murray as though he'd been there. 'Nowadays, everybody goes to town to die. And they just get cremated right there before you know it.' Keith started to ride slowly around them.

'Is he going to hell or heaven, Keith?' asked Doug.

'Hell, it looks like. He's too mean. Now he'll get what he deserves,' cried Keith. 'Come on, guys! We can have a race around the schoolhouse. What do you say?' They were too busy talking, so they ignored his request. 'Then I'll test it out myself.'

Murray waited until Keith was out of listening distance and whispered to Doug. 'My dad said that old man Cougar had to be a shark, a white one with gory teeth. And you know what,' he added, pretending to tell Doug a secret. 'He just popped up here like that one day. Nobody knows where old man Cougar comes from. He was picked up one day by a fishing boat.' He was trying to convince Doug.

'Old man Cougar, a shark? That's the dumbness thing I've ever heard,' he laughed without any control. 'A shark. Nay, a skunk. Wait,

I've a better one for you—a gold fish. No, an octopus.'

'As far as I'm concerned you don't know anything. My dad said old man Cougar's skin was like a shark's—all shiny and glittering. He doesn't even have any wrinkles like other men. When he went fishing, he always swam to shore. His partner, old Lewis, had to bring the boat back. Winter was nothing for him. That isn't all. My father said that old man Cougar never took a shark in. And if any boats caught one, old man would buy it from him, and then freed it. Yea, that old man Cougar is a shark lover. What, I'm telling you, is true, or God will strike me down dead on the spot.'

The Timeman stopped the scene, expecting Edwin to say something. And Edwin didn't miss that opportunity.

'Murray really has his feet in the ground. He sees our communities as gradually disappearing. The spirit of our community has been injured. Because life and death are anonymous in big cities. And my grandpa's death is an attempt to restore the community. The fiber that binds people together, even afterlife.

'And look at Doug. He knows very well that all of us are Christians. And Christianity tells us that the soul is an indestructible substance. Good ones go to Heaven. And bad ones to Hell. And he is telling Murray that though we all practice Christianity, we are somehow allowing our community to vanish. Because people see eternal blessing coming from God alone. So, they tolerate the destruction of communities as their suffering before our compassionate and merciful Christian God. But my grandpa isn't like that. Though he accepts *Eternal Blessing* because there isn't anything to lose in believing in God, he brings people back to the importance of community blessing, a pragmatic life with intrinsic values. Friendship is the essence of community soul.'

'Can we move on?' asked the Timeman.

'No!' Edwin replied, surprising his grandpa. 'You really think that their talks about animals are nonsense. You're wrong. Today's people have misplaced their sense of community. They are much more preoccupied with animals as though animals, in turn, can teach us about our deteriorating communities. If we participate in our own community spirit, animal rights will flourish. Actually, I don't know whether animals have souls. You should know this better than I. I think that if a cat or a dog has a lasting image, it might glitter in your time cell. And I've seen many blank ones.

'Because people passively watch their community disappearing, they prefer to hold the view that animals have souls. And they prefer the animal companion much more than the human one.' The Timeman didn't challenge Edwin, as they continued to observe the boys' conversation. 'Everybody knows that your father is dumb. He lost a net on the dock, capsized his boat on the shore, and crashed his boat on a school of herrings. He's jealous. Old man Cougar is the only person who got rich from fishing. But again, he's a shark. That's cool!'

'You talk about my father as dumb. Look at yours, he isn't any better. He's a cheater, a snake! He's stupid like old man Cougar.' Both of them stopped speaking for a few seconds until Keith passed them.

'And I guess your father told you that, too.'

'Everybody knows that.'

'Then tell Keith that old man Cougar is a shark if you want a bloody nose. Old man Cougar is cool. He put his net where there were sharks. And that's cool! Sharks go after fish, so the fish get themselves stuck in his net. That was his baby. He isn't like your deadbeat father who thinks that sharks only eat the fish off his net.'

'My dad said that there were always sharks near his boat. And on top of that, old man Cougar never caught a single one of them. How come?' Murray waited for Doug to say something, but he did not give him sufficient time. 'I say once and for all, he has to be a shark.'

'How stupid can you be? Nobody ever catches sharks around here except for your dad. Your dad didn't tell you that old man Cougar swam with sharks? Did he?' He didn't tell you why old man Cougar became rich from fishing?' He stared at Murray who was half a head shorter than he was—an odd ball.

'Yeah, you're so cool. You're the only person who thinks he knows everything around here. Just because your brother is studying to become a doctor, it doesn't make you smarter than anyone else. Mark my words. That Cougar is a shark man.'

'Who cares if he's a whale or a plant!' Doug's shouting attracted Keith's attention, but they changed the subject very quickly when Keith joined his friends again. 'What worries me is if dying is painful. The widower, James Crook, looked awful and cried like a baby. All the women and men tried to comfort him, but he wouldn't stop braying. I couldn't believe how he made everybody else cry after him. You see, dying has to be painful. But where is the pain? In the stomach? The head? Maybe, it's in the chest.' He waited for Keith to talk about his grandmother or grandfather's pain.

'It's painful. My dad said that when someone is about to die, the pain is like a lightning shock through the whole body. It squeezes out the soul from the body. It's more painful if a person has to go to hell. That's why a dying person messes his bed. Oh, it's torture! You couldn't imagine so much burning and squeezing pain. It's worst than having a roller flattening you out. My dad said that you could see it in the widower James' face. Widower James knew he was going straight to hell. But he didn't want to go, so he tired to hold back his soul. He had to suffer so much more. Finally, the devil won.' Murray nodded his head in an affirmation as though he had actually experienced death.

'Before my grandma died, I asked my mother why she was crying. She said that she didn't know why. And Grandma was sad and worried because Grandpa would be all alone. So she cried. Oh, I think it makes them feel good. It blocks out pain. You remember when we went into the school through the window and I ripped my leg? Look, the scar is still here. The stitches are only just gone now. When it happened, it was paining like hell. It was scary because of the bleeding. I thought I'd bleed to death. So I cried a tiny little bit. And when I did, I didn't feel any pain. And I wasn't scared either. It's all the same when I'm happy, sad, angry, or rolling with laughter. You see crying blocks off all pain. I wanted to act out my feelings for you all to see, so I cried. So, I cried some more to have my mind and body on the same level. You Doug! You got me grounded for one whole month without any allowances.' He squinted his eyes to show his penalty.

'One month, only!' cried Murray. 'All you had to do was stay at home like a prince. I was boxed in the house for six weeks. No TV, no snacks, no computer—nothing. I had to do all the dishes by hand. That wasn't all, I had to clean the toilet every week. At night I smelled like it. Oh, it wasn't only boring, but it was a real torture, especially the toilet smell.'

'Wow, Murray! That's cool! All that stuff for nothing,' interrupted Doug.

'And what did your parents do to you, Doug? It's your turn. Let's hear it.' He waited for him to answer.

'All I had to do was to break another window at home, so they could take it out from my allowance.'

'You're lying! Why don't you say the truth?' Murray asked angrily.

'I don't lie, biscuit brain!'

'You're like your father. You don't lie, really. Who told everyone we went in through the door that was left open. And then it closed behind us, so we'd to break the window to get out. Isn't that lying?'

'Why don't you ask your father, Murray? Anyway, Keith, is your grandpa starting to smell?'

'What are you driving at? Nothing is wrong with his nose,' answered Keith.

'The dying smell like rotten fish guts,' Murray replied, smiling.

'How should I know? Can't you see that I'm here?'

'Keith, is your grandpa still crying his head off?' asked Doug, wanting to hear about sufferance and the agony of dying.

'Crying? No. It's more like he's enjoying it. He doesn't have to pay for another bike. Oh, he's laughing all the way to hell with all his money,' Keith huffed impatiently.

'Wow, that's cool,' cried Doug. 'Maybe, he's going for a long and expensive trip. Gosh, he can see his future. I wish I could, too. With me, I don't know anything. Over one million things could happen to me right now, mostly troubles. I don't know if I'm going to break the school's window again, to go into the schoolhouse, to smoke, to fight, or who knows what.'

'As you can see Timeman, these boys have entertained several ideas about death. In some religions, people believe that animals can foresee a person's death. They warn and mourn near a house where a person is about to die. Animals can sense a person's impending death because death has a peculiar smell. But human beings don't want to detect such a scent.

'The ancient Egyptian buried their dead along with animals, servants, food, and jewelry. They believed in an afterlife and that their possessions would become very useful for them in their new realm. Today, with all our scientific knowledge, we can't predict a person's death. We can neither prepare for it nor run away from it. But we still live as though all of our tomorrows are knowable. And we're responsible to pay back our debts, to care for animals, and to safeguard our environment because there'll be a tomorrow. We prepare ourselves for our careers. For good jobs. For our retirement. But nobody says to himself—I'm preparing for my death. I should make a lot of friends. And when death comes, we say it's natural. And all this my brother is saying. If we aren't responsible for our death, we shouldn't be responsible for our life and what we have done to others or ourselves in society. But nobody accepts this. Keith is saying that we should bring death up front. I accept that I'll die. Now, I am learning to live and have as many friends as possible. Keith isn't ignorant about his future actions. The future for him is like death coming without any warning.' He thought that the Timeman would question him, but he didn't. His grandpa showed that he didn't understand the young generation. So the Timeman, Mr Cougar, and Edwin listened to the boys carefully.

'You meant gigantic troubles,' cried Murray. 'Like taking your brother's anatomy book to school, looking at filthy magazines in class, puncturing bikes, breaking into lockers, sticking centerfolds on walls, writing dirty jokes about teachers,' said Murray.

'Trouble always looks for me. I don't even know where it comes from. With all the wrong things I've done, I could line them off on the main road, one after another until they reach town.'

'Boy, you're going straight to hell when you die,' cried Murray. 'You even broke my bike, burnt my books. Look! Another one passing.' Everyone stared at the speeding white station wagon passing by with a huge logo on. 'That's City – TV racing by. Nothing ever happens here. Not so long ago, City – RS went by. There must be something big happening in Albion or Chesney, a fire or an accident.' These communities were much more populated than Sandreef.

'Wow, that's great! I guess we can check it out, Murray. Anyway, what is *RS*?'

'Radio Service, stupid! Everybody knows that. No, wait, the "S" is for station,' answered Murray.

'Listen guys, I have to head back. Maybe Marion is waiting for her bike,' cried Keith. He had a hunch that City – TV and RS were going to his place, so he sped away quickly.

'Doug, why don't we go to Albion? There's more action there, than in this dead place.'

'I'll race you,' yelled Doug, as he dashed ahead. Unfortunately, they would have a short race, for all roads led to the Cougars' that day.

'Timeman, I've a question for you,' Edwin said.

'What is it?' he asked.

'How many times have you listened to the boys' conversation? How many times did I make the same comment?'

'Keep on guessing. For your interest, you observe the most interesting events and happenings.'

'You're the lord of time. You can do anything you want with time. Perhaps these events have never taken place. Or, maybe they did. And you're just playing them back to me.' The Timeman didn't answer him. Edwin continued: 'You're my future adversary. You want to make me your victim. You can jump in and out of time as you wish. There isn't any past or future for you. You're trying to get me, but not my grandpa. Maybe he died a long time ago. Now, you're playing with my memory. Isn't that it?'

'Keep wondering,' replied the Timeman. They found themselves involved in other events.

13:30 Scotty and Edwin

As Keith hit the homeward bound road, he nearly collided into Scotty Bowman, who was a local alcoholic whose obnoxious odor surpassed any fishing industry. He never bathed and wore the same dirty clothes and shoes everyday. His hair, mostly gray and long to his neck, was glued together like electric wires. And yet, his long hair could not hide his dandruff. His swollen eyelids and puffy face peeped through his bushy beard. One thing always changed—the wine bottle, his vital prop in his hand. The one he had this day was less than half full.

'Excuse me Scotty, I nearly ran you over,' cried Keith, stopping at a fair distance from him.

'You said it, lad!' Scotty stammered in a thick voice. 'You want to damage my vital bottle.' Scotty was thrown into a talkative state. He took his other swollen hand with long black fingernails and clamped it around his bottle like a baby. With some continuously dripping sores on his swollen legs, he dragged his feet slowly on the road toward Keith.

'Guess what, Scotty! Grandpa is going to die, at four o'clock today...' He felt content to surprise Scotty.

Scotty looked around in the street and then at him, 'New bike, you got yourself?' He looked up in the thick blue sky which appeared to thin off, as it stretched to the horizon.

'Yeah, it's Marion's. I can use it today,' he joyfully cried, 'Isn't that neat?'

'Hmm, your grandpa should take some of my vital. It'd kick up some fire in him,' he said, staring at Keith dragging off swiftly.

Scotty often marched from one end of the street to the other at a steady speed, and his stride was synchronized and symmetrical with the pendulum motion of the wine bottle in his hand. Dragging himself for hours along the road, mumbling only to himself, keeping his head in a harness position, and leaving a black line on the road, he became Sandreef's standardized clock. Some people gave him used shoes rather than buying new clocks. During Scotty's walking state, most young boys shouted at him with vulgar insults; and yet, his ears were mostly immune to sound. His marching up and down hardly raised an adult's eyebrow, for his soul transpired as a windpipe to be played on by an unknown force. Often, when visitors passed through Sandreef, they thought everyone else in this little community resembled him, so they hurried away.

Most older people were kind to him except when he suddenly stumbled into his standing state, in which a statue suffered less than him. Mentally blocking off the immediate world around him, rendering everything around him helpless, blocking the road, and mildly disrupting everyone's ordinary life, and driving at both sides of him became a custom. Shouting, honking, yelling, screaming, and swearing: all were humbled before him. Sometimes, the daily fishing truck arrived late because he had blocked the road, and nobody wanted to take home his odor for several days. Luckily, he usually stood in one place for exactly four hours without moving or switching legs, and stared at his hand or a pebble. It was impossible to identify what he usually fixated on. And yet, the community's icon always wore a profound smile on his face while he grumbled and remained completely frozen, as though several thousand years ago had rolled over him. Calling community workers to move him merely added another paddle stroke on a wet surface.

In the freezing and long winter months, some people would throw an old blanket over him during his standing state; they usually put some food or money in his stretched hand that nobody could bend without breaking. When he woke up from his trance, he would use the money for another cheap bottle of wine. Several times he was hospitalized, especially for pneumonia and malnutrition; he often got transferred from one hospital to another in town. No psychiatric clinics allowed him to stay in for long, for his activities appeared to be preprogrammed, and the real cause for his conditions was a mystery. Because he was not a real danger to himself or others, he was quickly permitted to return to the street. Doctors said that he had a severe alcoholic problem that might have caused slight brain damage.

He seldom went to someone else's house to eat or sleep for the night; he would take their food, which was intentionally left outside for him, and eat it. He preferred to sleep in a boat cabin that had been left unlocked for him. With no intention of damaging another person's property, he could not stop his odor from lingering in a tiny cabin, and this made it very difficult for some people who cared for him. Though there were over fifty boats and garages, on rare occasions he slept in his haunted house that held a trace of being abandoned and without soul.

A few people said he had become like this because he had slight brain damage from nearly drowning. He'd fallen overboard during a stormy evening while he was putting out his fishing nets. He had been unconscious in the water, and was rescued too late. Some said he'd gone swimming while drunk. A handful believed that he had tried to commit suicide in the ocean. Others thought that because his wife and children had gone to another community nine years ago, he started to drink. And a very few thought that everything started after he had been imprisoned in town for drinking and fighting in a bar. He'd been locked up for the entire weekend without any bail. Some people had trouble believing that such a hideous thing could occur in their town, especially someone being badly beaten up and sexually abused in prison. Those believers thought of such an act as an everyday event in prison. And yet, those who made another person believe in any of these stories could make him live in absurdities. For all these years, he never revealed why he had become a local drunk. Alcohol had taken its course, and his stammering and slurring vocal pipe echoed his empty world.

From where he stood, he sniffed the air for the odor of death, and unconsciously fell into a momentarily trance. But he was quickly repelled to consciousness. A force stronger than his conscious effort took possession over his body—like being in a hypnotic state. His body then turned toward the direction of the ocean. And then his feet dragged along the paved road onward until he reached the narrow path between the Cougars' and Harris' houses. The salt water could not heal his old wounds. The blue sky held no suspicion, as its penetrating blueness played off any free spirit; dancers gracefully floated to ritual beats: the little petal in Scotty's life glittered in a new season.

A hundred meters away was the shore; the dry layer of sand on top could deceive strangers that it was the peak of summer. At midday, he did not expect to see anyone working on his boat or strolling by, and he forced his way against the weak wind. About twenty meters ahead, he noticed a figure sitting alone on the sand and staring at the waves playing off the dazzling sunlight. From the person's physical posture he knew that it had to be someone young.

He stopped a few meters behind him and recognized the face that gazed upon the blue horizon where silvery bubbles danced: 'A shark out there on the horizon,' he stammered in an attempt to start a conversation without imposing his presence. The stranger was nobody other than Edwin. 'Hmm, for a thousand years, I've been sleeping. I felt like...' he grumbled as though he'd finally found the spirit to live for. Barred from stretching his fragile body and searching out in his surroundings for the answer, Scotty saw some hope. On several occasions, he used to hear a voice in him saying that the terror of the sea, and the terror under the sea coming. And a strong urge within him appeared to be leading him to the ocean. He looked behind him and noticed his heavy feet had ploughed the sandy shore, exposing the wet layer of soil.

'Darn!' Scotty cried, being rigid with shock and stood lifelessly. Edwin was completely unaware of the spiritual transformation that had left Scotty's body like a stale corpse in the wind. The silence behind Edwin didn't heighten his loneliness and desperation; he didn't glance behind him and notice that Scotty wasn't sleeping, his wine bottle lying in the sand. Nobody could have forgotten Scotty's human repellent. 'I'm sorry. I didn't know that my trance is contagious,' Scotty said and stared at his wine bottle.

'Sorry son, this stuff could kill anyone,' Scotty said smiling. He continued to grumble as Edwin appeared to watch the empty ocean for a sign. 'My vital prop has already made me hollow. If it doesn't bother you, may I sit?' He patiently waited for Edwin's approval.

There was no answer. Clumsily, he tried to sit near him, but he fell heavily on his rear. Scotty sat and watched the rolling waves until his souls was combed around the sitting horizon, consuming him like a pipe for rolling waves to play off.

'I felt as though I'd been out of touch for ages,' he grumbled with a mouthful of wine. 'If I must say, I used to watch Ralph swim here. Right here, every evening.'

His revelation did not evoke any response, and Scotty got the message from the silent sufferer who was fumbling over his grandfather's secret.

'You can only observe and not interfere with events,' reminded the Timeman.

'At least, you should have allowed me to see him coming. Why are you interested in him, anyway?'

'Interested, no. Haven't you noticed life and death in him?'

'No, he's still alive.'

'In his trances, he entertains images like being confined to a time cell. He can't change what he sees. He's away from the world of the living. Death is like being a passive spectator who can't influence anything. People are bestowed with a useless soul.'

'Although you may know how to make a soul a prisoner, you are still unable to destroy it. There're mysteries that lie behind our souls. And Scotty reminds me of those mysteries in life and after life. We know that Scotty lives in the pit. And yet, his world is unknown to us. I don't know how he thinks.'

'He merely entertains images and doesn't think,' the Timeman remarked.

'Scotty represents a criticism of our flourishing lifestyle. His situation has awakened many of us in our community. We treat him with enthusiasm. And share whatever we have. He makes me realize the essence of my life. It's unfortunate that he had to suffer so much.'

'How could that miserable wretch have a community soul?'

'Nowadays, some people need evidence of how short life is. Scotty makes us see with our heart. When I look at him, my heart softens. And if I could reverse his situation, I wouldn't hesitate for a second. How I feel toward him comes from the community soul in us.'

'You've forgotten something. In life, people paint their images. And after life, they live in their images.'

'As far as I know, from Scotty's lifestyle, I have learned a lot. Grandpa, you aren't saying anything,' he asked for help. Mr Cougar did not say anything.

'Ralph, look at the horror that you have created,' cried the Timeman.

13:45 Cougar's House

Within just a short time, individuality found collectivity like a pack of sheep searching outward for their missing king. All bleating was neatly combed in to place in the little arc street that is nearest to the ocean is Cougar's house. One could have easy access to the roaring blue ocean. And his house, which was newly renovated and enlarged to make it the biggest one in the street, is quite noticeable from a distance. Both ends of the street branch off to the main road that passes through Sandreef. In that short street, numerous cars, vans, motorbikes, and bicycles parted on both sides of the street. Most of these vehicles came from nearby communities and from town, leaving a narrow passage for traffic.

In the street, the most spectacular scene was the local police, Harry-James King. Wearing his uniform, which was still new, he gave others the inspiration that everything was under control and humbly displayed his shining honor banner on his jacket. Conscientious observers crowded around him, for they wanted to hear his tales of how Mr Cougar was an ideal citizen. The boys, Keith, Doug, and Murray also assisted the police in his endeavor, in a less serious way.

From the crowd, it appeared as though some people felt there was occasion to exhibit their wardrobes today; a few were exchanging and comparing notes about human closeness with town inhabitants to see whether certain feelings of sadness still had value. And yet, most of them were here to reinforce their sense of community in human beings: that the essence of living could be found in collectivity. The crowd grew, and bigger groups were near the house where City – RS and TV had parked their vans in front of Mr Cougar's house.

Mr King's optimism about Mr Cougar's promise radiated in people's minds, and he told them that nobody should consider himself as a stranger in Sandreef. He spoke about the tone of community crying out from Mr Cougar's house, which brought observers to their knees.

'My grandpa's soul will shine. It will live forever in everyone's mind,' Edwin interrupted the continuation of events. 'People from our community have molded my grandpa. They're all coming over to honor my grandpa's worthwhile life. In this way we will overcome your reality of death. My grandpa's soul is an extra social object, the intrinsic value between him and his community. And these people around our house will uphold his deeds after his death,' he said, feeling overwhelmed by the crowd outside.

'Your confidence is running high—only for me to feed on it. Ralph can't die. We had this out before. Nothing exists outside of time. Now, enjoy what is transpiring in the house.'

The entire yard was already crowded with mourners. On the sidewalks, people were also standing in line for a glance of Mr Cougar who had mystically grasped them like a voice in the wind: a voice that could command death in a few hours. It was difficult to bypass some stagnant mourners crowding the entrance to Mr Cougar's front door. Lewis stood like a lonely soldier up against an opposing army near the door. Though some observers knew the patient well and had already given their condolences, Lewis' face said it all: like an ecclesiastic scale as being too limited to register his misery, pain, and indignant agony. He threw out the aroma of a withdrawn creature that was too poor to acknowledge confirmed sentimentalists. And yet, a righteous refinement that hovered near the scene and betrayed the shades of life to take on brilliant colors that reflected human moods suppressed the mystery of dying and the unexpected that often came in gloomy obscurity to match mourners' uninspired clothes.

Once visitors passed the door, the huge living room was agreeable to their sense of spaciousness. Near the inside stairs were three bedrooms and the washroom; on the left, the kitchen faced the ocean, and the living room window opened toward the road. Mr Cougar, who was lying in his single bed with its head toward the window, could see everything that happened in his living room and kitchen. The doctor sat next to him. All the chairs from Catherine's apartment were against the walls. Catherine, Marion, and Richard were on the sofa. Some mourners stood along the walls and in the kitchen; others were comfortably sitting on the floor.

Radio people were in the living room, too. At first, an announcer at the station jokingly and dramatically exaggerated the initial tip in his broadcast. Their director, hearing it and thinking that this was big news around here, quickly dispatched a team to verify, to transmit current development, and to interview family members, as well as the actual patients. The radio announcer, Mr Wright, a middle aged man, was overworking some neighbors in the kitchen. Until now the radio broadcasting was trying to stretch its audience's imagination to an unexplored periphery.

People are not accustomed to listening to radio and looking at television at the same time. TV stations often monitor radio stations for tips, and City – TV quickly sent his team to broadcast Mr Cougar's tragedy, grief, and the dignified act of dying. The team was also interviewing and interpreting emotional sensationalists who expressed strong overtones about Mr Cougar's tragedy. Until now, it was filming the crowd outside, mourners inside, and some who were interviewing. City TV's anchorwoman, Romie Cook, had arrived. She was one of the best reporters who could intuitively draw the line between facts and pain, public knowledge and personal integrity, and interrogation and inviting voluntary answers. Besides her professionalism, she was a beautiful woman in her late twenties, with wavy blonde hair like a calm stream with sparkling green stones, black eyelashes and eyebrows that would demystified nights, a concave nose for roses and fragrances, fully round lips to match her generous nature, and breasts, hips, and legs that spoke volumes of poetry. Her fine tanned skin showed life and she was like a human magnet radiating to attract. All this went with her hypnotic voice that could lure the deaf and dumb. Her cameraperson often suffered from lack of concentration and had to be replaced periodically. Besides all this, she received about a vanload of flowers from secret admirers every week. The town of Rose Hall, where she was born, forged her coming. Today, the remaining wild beasts and dodo birds on the horizon were in for a comprehensive stimulation.

She surveyed everyone in the living room with a half smile, deceiving them into thinking that she was politely saying hello and humbly acknowledging their grievance, knowing that their thoughts could not go beyond their actual experience of seeing and smelling her in the same room. She was looking for the right sentiment; one that was not overcast with profound grief and pain, but one that would stand out among the crowd for the viewers. She chose Marion, who was sitting near her mother with her ghostly air, and impenetrable depth in her eyes that foretold a passionate attempt to unravel this mystery. As she oozed toward her, Marion heeded to the cameraman's signal to stand up so that he could have a half shot of her.

'Marion, I'm sorry about your unbearable suffering and unimaginable grief at this moment, and no one could experience such emotional pain,' humbled the reporter, as she carefully followed Marion's movement to grasp whether she could be directed to the present. Marion nodded her head in acknowledgement. 'You're Marion Morris, Mr Cougar's granddaughter, aren't you?'

'Yes.'

'You saw your grandfather earlier this morning, isn't that so? But he didn't give you any sign, no indication whatsoever that he'd be passing away today? Did he?'

'No, he didn't.'

'Did he look the same this morning as he does now?'

'No.'

'He's much older, now. How much would you say—five or ten years?' she recognized that Marion would not divulge any additional information unless she was asked to.

'Grandpa gets older every minute.'

'It must be very shocking for you, wouldn't you say so?'

'It's incredible. You wouldn't believe it, Miss Cook,' Marion stammered, reminding the reporter of this incomprehensible phenomenon, 'Grandpa looks all dried up now. He's much older and grayer too. His voice even sounds older. In the morning, he didn't look like this. He was cleanly shaven and had very short hair. Now look. You can hardly recognize him.'

'Thank you very much Marion, and I do sympathize with your agony.' She turned to face the camera. 'You've heard it from a direct eyewitness. Within a few hours, Mr Cougar has aged about ten years. Is it natural? Or unnatural? We're confronted with a real mystery. Does Mr Cougar know exactly when he will die?' The camera took a close up of the patient along with the mourners in the room. The mourners' dreadful predicament and confusion could not be easily wiped away with Kleenex and handkerchief. Miss Cook realized that she had to mingle with people who were feeling with a similar sympathy and tried not to be an imposter with an unscrupulous agenda of agitating others' grief with offensive questions in this extremely sensitive situation. The skillful and highly experienced middle aged cameraman went down on his knees to capture a half image of Catherine who was mostly silent and who tried to endure her suffering internally. She could not control certain physical symptoms: her bloating face, moist eyes, trembling chin and hands, and an emptiness that barely held her vacant body together. Miss Cook synchronized herself to her team; she said a few words into the microphone and then cried, 'Here, we've Mr Cougar's daughter, Mrs Morris, in view.' Catherine appeared as though she was desperately trying to escape publicity. 'Mrs Morris, you live in the same house. If I'm not wrong, you live on the second floor. And your father lives on this one.'

Catherine stared at her blankly, then nodded her head in agreement. 'I'm truly sorry, but for our viewers, I have to ask you a few questions, if you don't mind.' She waited for eye contact with Catherine. 'You were absolutely shocked when your father told you about his faith, at exactly twelve o'clock today.'

'Yes. But you people wouldn't understand it,' she murmured. Like a fox without his grapes, Richard naturally rescued his wife from the unfriendly interrogation by putting his arm on her shoulder. She hid her face in her arms while Richard blocked the camera from filming her.

'Family members are deeply shocked by this unfortunate event that is unfolding in Sandreef,' she continued, briefly interrupted by another team member who came in with a camerawoman.

'We need one more camera to take a constant image of the patient's deteriorating condition for the office,' whispered the technician. Without losing any time, the other camera was operational at the side of the bed where the doctor was. Miss Cook went to the family doctor who was sitting near his patient controlling the I.V.

'Excuse me, Dr Robinson,' he turned and smiled into the camera as though he was caught unaware. But he could not stand it any longer, in this room where he disagreed with the interrogation. He believed that all of the medical questions should be directed to him. He was relieved when asked, 'We'd like to ask you some questions about your patient's health.' Content to respond to her demand, as he moved a few meters away from the patient.

'Yes, what can I do for you?' he asked softly.

'You've seen Mr Cougar only yesterday in the street. And you've been his personal physician for several years now, haven't you?'

'Yes, I have. If you want to know, Miss Cook, my patient hasn't suffered from any sicknesses, besides the ordinary cold like any of us. He's in impeccable health. He has no disease or mental problem. He's stronger than an elephant.'

'You're saying that you've an up-to-date medical file. And Mr Cougar sees his physician regularly.'

'Not exactly, my fair-lady. Excuse me, I meant my dear lady!' giggling at himself for the slip of the tongue. 'Yes, what am I saying? I'm your fan. I look at you everyday on TV...'

'Thank you, sir. Your patient, Mr Cougar, please.'

'Yes, as I was telling you, patients see their doctor mostly when they're sick. The last time he came in was over nine months ago for a complete medical checkup. He didn't have a scratch on him!' he said, smiling carelessly like a little boy with butterflies in his heart.

'In other words, you're saying Mr Cougar is in perfect health.'

'Only yesterday I saw him in the street. Isn't that something? It's a small community here. Everybody knows each other here. You couldn't miss anyone. It isn't like a town where a doctor has to consult his medical charts first to know whether this is the same patient he treated the day before.' Though he appeared to be absent minded about the truth of his patient's dying, he still assured the reporter about his sound judgment, especially concerning medical matter and social issues in his community.

'Are you saying that yesterday he didn't look the way he does now? Can you please tell us how he was physically yesterday?'

'As I said before - he was in perfect health; he was in good spirits, and everything seemed to be under control.'

'Would you say his physical appearance is the same as yesterday?'

'Well, he didn't look so old. As a matter of fact, nobody looks older than him. From yesterday to now, it seems as though I haven't seen him for ages.'

'You're saying he's aged a lot and has more wrinkles.'

'Well, I'd say so, physically, mind you.'

'Were you shocked when you first saw him today?'

'Not shocked. If I must say, I was completely taken in to keep the record straight. I though at first he was someone else. But Ralph couldn't trick me.' The doctor could not hide his blushing when he had eye contact with her.

'What do you mean by saying Mr Cougar looked like someone else, doctor?'

'Oh, I didn't tell you yet. His body liquid started to dry up rapidly. So I've given him a liquid solution. He's already had about three bags of solution. And I don't have anymore in stock.'

'Why didn't you send him to the hospital for treatment?'

'He didn't want to go to the hospital. It's a place for sick people, not for my patient. He wants to say goodbye to his friends, here.'

'According to your judgment, you've been here for about an hour. Would you say that he's been aging about one year every fifteen minutes or so?'

'Well, I'm not into speculation. I don't want to make unfounded guesses. We need facts, hard data.'

'But he looks older since you've been here? Wouldn't you say so?'

'Well, this isn't a medical judgment, a personal one. Yes! With due respect Miss Cook,' staring at her from head to toe, 'everybody in here can see it. Why can't you?'

'Doctor, are your patient's vital signs normal?'

'Yes, his pulse is OK. His blood pressure is in order. His heart beat is normal and regular, too.'

'One last question doctor if you don't mind. How did you react when Mr Cougar told you that he was going to die at exactly four o'clock?'

He looked around the room for a place to escape; regrettably, there was none. He noticed that the clock on the wall was about five minutes slow. 'Catherine has said it all. You couldn't understand. Ralph helped to build our clinic here. Everybody loves him, and he has never hurt a fly. He loves all of us dearly. To lose his love, it makes this community empty, hollow. It'd be a great loss to mankind. Mind you, there isn't anything medically or mentally wrong with him. It's just tragic. You'd better look around Madame. Everyone can see his kindness, his generosity, his good sense of humor, his friendship, and his compassion.... I am to respect his word, and his destiny, too. It's very sad; it's a pity.' He wiped his eyes with his handkerchief, for the grief was unbearable when he spoke about his personal relationship with his patient and dearest friend. Feeling subdued, he walked away from the camera to his post and sat.

'Thank you, doctor,' mumbled the reporter, as she quickly dashed to the washroom to rearrange her posture. The encounter had been too strong for her to remain objective; she too felt as though she was about to lose a dear friend who she had known over the ages.

'I've seen it all. It's quite clear to me that you want to pass me off as mentally deficient,' objected Mr Cougar when he looked at his body.

'You are the one who told everyone to come to your funeral. I've empowered your body with fear and uncertainty. For some of you, your biological clocks work much faster than others. The results are remarkable. Don't try to second guess my nature.'

'Which part of my grandpa isn't real?' Edwin asked the Timeman.

'It's clear to me you could easily abolish my grandpa's consciousness from his body along with his knowledge of it.'

'You're learning quickly,' he answered.

'Thanks. Is it that my grandpa had already passed away? And it was I who was lying in the bed? Maybe I'm lying in my dying bed. And I'm recollecting my failure as though it were only yesterday,' Edwin murmured, feeling uncertain about his own nature. He thought that he wouldn't get a straight answer. The Timeman responded:

'The lord of time is multi-dimensional, not one-dimensional. While you're here to save Ralph, you must learn about my nature, but not yours,' replied the Timeman, and other events were indirectly informing Edwin and Mr Cougar to observe keenly.

14:00 Mr Cougar's Testimony

A police helicopter hovered steadily in the sky. The time was drawing nearer, and the crowd was growing larger around the community. People from nearby communities and Rose Hall took the front row. All told the story of deserted houses and the manifestation of the community in man. Thousands of vehicles were already parked in every conceivable place in Sandreef. Some commuters had abandoned their cars along the main road and continued on foot; they all wanted to be where human solidarity was unfolding before the last frontier of life where they wished to have a glimpse of their own destiny. The mayor and other top officials from town mingled among mourners and local residents, because to will death was unrealistic. Another police helicopter landed in the field near the schoolhouse, where there were already a dozen of these vehicles: four from the police department; four from journalists; and four VIPs.

Another unmarked helicopter came into view in the open sky and filmed the crowded streets and gardens to show how families and strangers could peacefully assemble together without exchanging gifts. Most people, hoping to have a quick view of Mr Cougar, were content with actually being at the scene with others. Some of them brought their own TV to have the latest; some were glued to their car or pocket radios. And yet, others enthusiastically went to some local residents for a comfortable view of the threading of events. Sandreef had new life. Whenever something new occurred, it radiated like pollen in the wind. To make sure that people ate "pure meat," journalists from TV stations, radio stations, magazines, and newspapers installed themselves in the crowd. Though it was extremely difficult for them to have the right people to interview, they were not completely grounded in thick mud.

Though Mr Cougar's street was getting over crowded and earlier sympathizers still remained near the house, those with wheelchairs, those who were mentally handicapped, or with other diseases forced themselves through the crowded streets. This was their last hope of being cured of their illnesses for their sickness, as their family members believed that Mr Cougar was holy and could cure any ailment. Police from Rose Hall had been directing the human traffic and struggling dexterously to keep a hairline passage free near the house so that these people would not miss their chance. And yet, the general sentiment was that it did not really matter whether Mr Cougar lived or died, for anything around him was considered sacred, including the street.

In the house, the anchorwoman hurried back to the scene, refreshed now without appearing like a bitter mourner. She was searching the vicinity for Betty who had put on a dramatic show for Mr Wright. Betty was exhibiting her deep love toward her father. Her display, her immeasurable feast of love drove her unconsciously toward complete exhaustion; she was now in the bedroom with a handful of local residents who were trying to resurrect her from her bitter ordeal.

'Let's go and find Betty,' Miss Cook told her regular; he went to look for her.

Miss Cook hesitantly walked toward the bed in which Mr Cougar was lying; the bed head was about twenty-degrees upward; she was uncomfortable because she did not know what to expect, and how to ask a dying man questions. As she pondered about what sort of questions to ask him and waited for her cameraman, the doctor told Miss Cook about Betty's helpless faith. She thought it would be easier to express her grievance like others visitors, and then she quickly remembered what Catherine had said about *not understanding anything*. Miss Cook was just standing there by Mr Cougar's side and glancing at his face while he listened and nodded to newcomers. She thought, *He's very much conscious, and he's busy saying farewell to the continuous line of newcomers and friends that are coming to see him, one after the other. Look how he smiles and nods his head in acknowledgement, without speaking a word. Why do most mourners touch his shoulder or feet with sympathy and assurance as though everything would be OK?*

She was working and reworking herself to ask the right questions, but she couldn't get them out. She was completely speechless as Mr Cougar turned to the other side where the camera was filming and glanced at the reporter. He gave her a friendly smile, 'Don't look at me like that. Life can't be loose pages blowing in the wind with others gathering them and reading off your destiny. My dear young lady,' he said, giving her a friendly smile, 'we don't have much time.' He spoke quite distinctively and coherently with a heavy coarseness in his voice.

'Hum, Mr Cougar. If you don't mind me asking. How do you feel right now?'

'And you are, please?'

'We're from City-TV. And I'm Miss Cook.'

'In that case, Miss Cook. The best defense is ignorance.' It was apparent that the patient did not fully understand his own physical and mental states.

'I don't really understand, sir,' said Miss Cook, gaining a little confidence in herself.

'You see. When I look into the future, it chases me to despair. And the past shows me only atrocities.' He could not reveal how his battle with the Timeman would turn out. At least, he held a losing card.

'Sir, I can't understand you. You're speaking in riddles.'

'Young lady, you couldn't be any more beautiful. It's a waste to only cherish such rareness without really enjoying it. Get a person to be near you and then atrocities could become his destiny. It's only our beliefs that separate us from the beast.' She looked at him as he quickly felt into a brief sleep. He drifted further internally into it, but after only a minute, he quickly came back to consciousness, with a smile.

'Mr Cougar, are you still with us? You've been dozing on and off.'

'I guess so.'

'Can you tell us something about death? Many people would like to have some insight into it, and you appear to have a clear idea about it, sir,' she asked hesitantly.

'Death isn't it saying farewell to everyone who has made my life so meaningful. They've given me a purpose. And when I honestly live for this my life is free. Yes, life makes a bang! Dying, young lady is the most creative act, so be prudent with life.'

'Excuse me, sir,' she said, showing some respect for Mr Cougar who seemed to be wiser in the domain of death. 'Are you saying we can't die without a body nor live without a mind – or something like that?' Her soft voice made the patient light up.

This made her relinquish her unconscious self-defense against people who tried to take the upper hand in an interview. 'How do you know for sure that you'll past away at exactly four o'clock?' Some mourners in the room thought of her as an unwelcome and disrespected intruder after this irreverent question. Luckily these mourners did not want to act violently before the patient, so their strong emotion did not propel a spinning coin in the air for long.

The patient saw that his friends were offended and then said, 'People neither chase life nor death. Life chooses you, and death takes life. Nothing could take away my friends and family. Not my good deeds, nor the bad ones. I know how to live my life, so that my own death could be understood—the principle of how to live.'

'Thank you, sir.' Miss Cook looked around the room and saw that the mourners did not find any of this amusing. 'Is there life after death, sir?'

'Ask our doctor. He's a warm fellow, but he drinks too much these days. But again, you're asking me to answer if there are more deaths after this death: one for my body, one for my mind, one for my shadow, one for my ghost, one in each world. I don't know what to say. Ask the Timeman this question! He can tell you whether there are more deaths after this one.'

'Who is the Timeman?'

'Young lady. You can use most kinds of wood to make a fire. One makes a lot of smoke. Another gives off a little flame. Some continuously blaze, and some burn up too quickly. Others take a long time without you being able to see its intensity. Most of us use all of them together, and then we try to have a pure fire burning. Or, at least, somebody else adding pieces of wood to your fire. If you believe that there's a little flame burning in you,' speaking directly to the reporter, 'then that's it.' She was content to be treated personally, and not just as a professional reporter. He tried to tell about the principle of her soul as the essence of living.

'Mr Cougar! What will be the cause of your death?'

'Are you telling me life is a disease, and death is the cure?'

'In your medical report, we've to say what you die of, don't we?'

'Don't they usually do this after, not before?' he answered cheerfully as he stared at the doctor. 'If you want to know, I don't have a contract out on myself. Death is much more than the totality of life, my dear child. Others still keep us alive, long after we're gone. I die as I know how to live. Knowing the cause of death tells us how people have already lived and died.'

'Are you going to die naturally?' she inquired.

'You mean to tell me you don't care about my family and friends at my side? After my death, my love ones will keep my soul alive in their hearts.'

'I don't mean to be disrespectful, but why do some people call you the shark-man around here?'

'Look at you! You're so gorgeous and respectful, too. You've shown a strong sense of being polite to me. But you still have to do your job. People want you to get them the most relevant information about me. Everyday you work on yourself to be decent and fair toward others, and to do your job well. Sharks are like human beings in many ways. They're gentle and eloquent. They swim very gracefully, too. Oh, yes, they're highly respectful. With its nature and potential to get food, the graceful side is easily missed in the deep.' He sipped a glass of apple juice that was next to him on a small table, wetting his dry throat, and preparing himself to say some more, when he saw Keith burst in and sit near his mother. Catherine forced him to go and say hello to his grandpa, but he refused. Everyone in the room was abruptly interrupted when Richard screamed at Keith who did not want to say hello to his grandfather.

'When a swimmer sees a fin in the ocean, it's a horror and he panics. He kills himself first with his own fear, because the fin tells him what could happen. The fin also tells us a story of life, the direction of a life. So, whenever I see a fin, I see the direction of how to live with my family and others. And I'm contented with how I am and what I have.' Because of Mr Cougar's mental faculties, some people were profoundly worried as to whether he would really die in a few hours, for there were hardly any signs coming from him: no fear, no struggle for life, and no loneliness and suffering.

'Keith, come son,' cried the patient hoarsely. Slowly, with his hands in his pockets and swaying his body bashfully, Keith came.

'Thank you again Mr Cougar for this interview. Good luck, sir,' she said honestly, for she did not want to speak to Keith, and she needed a break for a moment from this dense environment that affected her concentration. 'That was Mr Cougar speaking. Be your own judge. Does the voice you just heard come from a person who is about to die?'

'You didn't give me a bike! But you give Marion one!' Keith painfully murmured in the room as his parents listened, knowing that they could hardly keep up with children's demand these days.

'Keith, Keith! You're too much in a hurry for a bicycle. You need a moped. I ordered a moped for you. Edwin will pick it up for you.'

'You really mean it? I'll get a moped?' He hugged his grandfather with joy as everyone keenly observed Keith's natural transformation. 'Did you hear that Marion? I'm getting a moped! I can't believe it. Edwin! Where's Edwin?' He looked around the room. 'You wait till Doug and Murray hear this one,' he continued. Seeing only sour faces in the room and that nobody was interested in his moped, he rushed off to find his friends who were clowning around with the crowd outside; he nearly ran into a policeman who was escorting a team of medical people with "Rose Hall General Hospital" written on their badges, bags, and some large cases.

Miss Cook's break was quickly terminated as everyone was staring at the small group of newcomers. They went straight to the patient as though he was an ordinary household object that the newcomers had returned to its place in the middle of the room. Leaving everyone in surprise, a newcomer cried, 'You must be Doctor Robinson,' as the family physician instinctively guarded his patient's right and dignity near him against unauthorized intervention.

'I'm Dr Watts, and these are my assistants and technicians. We're here to do some monitoring and conduct an examination. Can we speak to a family member, please?' he asked confidently. Mr Cougar was listening to him attentively, and the anchorwoman suspected that this intervention was authorized by the provincial judge, or else they would look silly doing this.

She interrupted abruptly, 'We're from City-TV, Dr Watts. Do you have any legal permission for examining the patient?' Though the doctor could not believe himself being next to such a beautiful woman, his medical integrity in public subdued advancement.

'Yes, we do! From the judge himself,' he said, showing the court order to the camera while it focused on the content.

'It says to treat the patient, Ralph Cougar, not to move him. And to treat the patient you need the patient's consent or family's permission. Doctor, do you usually make house visits? Does Mr Cougar have a contagious disease? Is his sickness a threat to society?'

'No. But this is an exceptional case. We're just following this court order, Miss Cook.'

'Who told the court to intervene, doctor?'

'Sorry, I don't know,' he blushed.

'Who would then?'

With a lot of self-discipline, the doctor managed to ignore her for a while. 'We'd like to put up a monitor to register his temperature. His blood pressure and pulse rate. Also, we want to take a few blood and urine samples. And we have some more IV bags with us.'

'Well, this is tolerable,' cried Dr Robinson, as he glanced at the patient and then at Mr and Mrs Morris for their implicit agreement. Tapping his patient's shoulder in acknowledgement of a routine task did not go unnoticed in the room. His family doctor could not easily overcome his desire to acquire some more medical knowledge with moderation, like using friendly sciences to dethrone old superstitions about the soul and afterlife. And having scientific data meant removing falsities rather than seeking the truth, like looking for an onion's core while threading the layers off one by one. The crowd in the room was getting restless and agitated, for everyone was waiting for the patient to defend himself against this degradation. They did not accept the presence of these medical people because they were uninvited. They devalued the mourners' self-worth and intrinsic values—the union among friends. Mr Cougar closed his eyes for a moment, for this unwelcome excitement was beyond his control, and all this had a life of its own which could not be trapped in a bottle. The technicians moved his bed further away from the inner wall and placed their instruments (a cardiac machine monitoring his heart-beat graphically and digitally, another machine showing his pulse rates, blood pressures, and temperature) beside him. All this decreed out a typical hospital room without any oxygen outlets on the wall, and it defeated the idea of acknowledging the existence of community soul.

'Cougar! Cougar!' Curious mourners standing in Mr Cougar's street and in neighbors' yards were shouting. Not allowing him to die in dignity gave rise to the slogan chanting that could transform the crowd to a rioting mob. The protest against medical treatments was born quickly, and it swept from one street to another. People from distance streets were forcing themselves closer to the scene. A journalist on the helicopter estimated that there were over twenty thousand people in Sandreef; all of them were participating in this ordeal. For the right fuel had transformed passive mourners to active protestors without the intention of damaging anything or hurting anybody. The entire house was vibrating from the protestors' screaming. The yelling crowd could not advance any further. Luckily, there were no riot squads to add fuel to the burning flame. Mourners in the house were gripped with fear and were thinking about their personal security, for they had found themselves in the middle of an exploding situation. The anchorwoman appeared to enjoy this new development for Mr Cougar's sake; and yet, her sense of self-preservation could not carry her away from here. The helicopter hovering overhead described the scene as being uncontrollable, like a huge mob with a single voice. For nothing like this could have been foreseen, and to prevent the worst from happening would involve being sensitive to the protestors' point of view.

Since the protestors recognized that they had made their point, their motto slowly died down. They returned to their passive state of mourning by sitting where they were and lighting candles and lighters. They believed in Mr Cougar's natural endeavor and hoped that he would not be taken as a fake, regardless of any medical intervention.

Inside, they were just about to remove the screen around the bed; the medical people had already gotten their samples—four tubes of blood and a half cup of urine. Most mourners in the room quickly learned to compare seeing the actual patient in bed with flashing green figures that continuously fluctuated within the normal range on the monitors. Then the patient opened his eyes and could slightly detect the sensors on his chest and hands. 'I don't mean to be rude, sir. I'd prefer if there was only one person here,' he said, glancing at Dr Watts who had just witnessed how ugly the crowd could be, knowing that the wish of a dying person could not be considered as an extra burden.

'Not all of us will stay here, only Doctor Bristol, sir. On behalf of the hospital, we wish you the best of health, and hope to see you well again.' Feeling very honored to be in his service, Dr Watts and his other colleagues, including the police, made for the front door.

'Excuse me, Dr Watts. I've been in this sort of situation before. From what I've seen outside a few moments ago, I suggest that you don't go out. Go upstairs and stay out of sight. You can take this policeman with you, too.'

'Thank you for your impeccable insight and experience. We'll just do that. One can never tell nowadays about a mob outside.' Dr Watts felt a little embarrassed at himself for having been so naïve and not realizing any future consequences of his actions. 'Yes, going outside would be sufficient enough to turn those mourners to a lynching mob,' he said, and they quickly went upstairs.

The reporter turned and faced the patient, as both of their eyes exchanged friendly approval, 'Sir, your health seems to be normal. The medical people put a new clock on the wall to show the correct time. Are you sure it'll be four o'clock? Not one minute before or after?' She felt very comfortable with Mr Cougar, like an old friend sharing mutual respect over the years.

'You're an angel, just like my Catherine! Why don't you look for a more dignified job rather than terrorizing and tormenting the little I have for myself?' Some mourners in the room started to grumble, for she had deliberately insulted the patient and would have to pay for it; and yet, they did not show any physical aggression toward her. 'It's better that you ask my old pal, Lewis. He's furious at me, totally upset. Look at him, how he's standing and holding up my destiny without yelling at me. Look, he's giving me another one of those perplexing looks again. He doesn't want me to die.'

People who knew Lewis saw him as a loner who was just doing time. Lewis stared at the mourners in the room, as he released a strong pouf of air from his mouth like exhaling their obnoxious odor. Unlike everyone else, his long oily hair went with his lumberjack shirt, brown pants, and a pair of boots. Obviously, he didn't have any time to prepare himself for a crowd, but he was listening attentively to their conversation.

'Yes, I see him, but he looks very angry with everybody. So, will it be four?' said the reporter.

'We've a lot of predictions and superstitions around: the number three, seven, thirteen, the four sixes, at midnight, under a ladder, a black cat, a shark …' Mr Cougar murmured and then grumbled himself into an unconscious state. Everyone was alarmed. Catherine covered her face with both hands and wept loudly. The monitors displayed normal vitals, for he was still alive. Some mourners thought that he had fallen into another coma, and that the end was much nearer than they had anticipated. The anchorwoman felt extremely sorry for pushing him so much, because her career has a life on its own, and it fluctuated like the stock exchange. She was looking for a job at the national broadcasting station and wanted to be known nationally: to have her name in everyone's home, to have sufficient wealth; to be invited by political leaders and celebrity; to be a top international journalist; and to read the evening news from anywhere in the world. Her brief solidarity with a person, Mr Cougar, who trusted her and accepted her wholeheartedly like a friend, would fade away as she betrayed him because of her career and her egoistic greed. She felt depressed and alone in the room without any friends.

While the camera bled over the mourners in the living room, she joined Catherine. Marion stood up and offered her a seat. Miss Cook could see how Catherine felt about losing her dear father, a true friend and a guardian of hope. Something inexplicable was burning in her; it could rip any heart into absolute confusion. She held Catherine's hand and squeezed it tightly in an effort to demystify each other's miserable feelings and emptiness.

'He's one of the bravest men to walk on this earth,' Miss Cook said. 'No one will be as brave and courageous as he is. He doesn't have any pride, no regrets, no sorrow, no bitterness, and no loneliness. Only joy and happiness, just being with his own family and friends. He must be very dear and special to you. I'd miss him, too.... I can't believe myself saying all this to you, I hardly know your father. I just met him. But it doesn't seem so to me. All this is incomprehensible, and now I'm expressing my sadness and sentiment in public.' Catherine took her other hand and gracefully put it over Miss Cook's.

'Yes, so virtuous and noble. I don't even know who to pray for. I don't want him to die. I love him too dearly. If I could take his place, I would. What would people say now, if he didn't pass away? Tell me, reporter woman? Should I pray for his death? Or for his recovery? What shall it be tomorrow? Should I get a new hairstyle, buy different cosmetics, new clothes, move to a big city? Plastic surgery would do, wouldn't it? Honestly, I don't understand anything. Nothing! Why couldn't he be like everybody else? Oh, God! Help me! Why did a mouse have to roar like a lion? Oh, I feel like a boat on its belly against the tide,' Catherine glanced upward as her cry bounced back to her. Her unbearable suffering, anguish, and distress could not echo in the wind. Nobody could soothe her and show her a way out of her conflicting feelings. The reporter appeared to be sympathetic, for she had also tasted conflict and bewilderment. While squeezing Catherine's hand tighter, she thought that being here was not the best decision in her life; and yet, she knew that she could not wipe her sorrow off so easily because Mr Cougar had already affected her internally. So she quickly adjusted herself and went straight to the private room to reaffirm herself.

'Listen, Romie! I'm talking to you," Miss Cook said to herself. 'Are you listening? Romie, Romie, you're a reporter. Yes, Romie, you're a professional – intelligent, sensitive, and attractive. Now, act like how everybody wants you to be. I say act! Be one with yourself. Be objective, too,' she spoke to herself. She quickly glanced at her watch and believed that she was not the only person controlling the time. 'My God, the time is flying. Come on Romie! Everything is happening so fast. Hurry! Hurry, hurry up—will you? Ready to face it, Romie? Calm down!' She looked at herself in the mirror and pointed at her reflection. To refresh herself, she took some cold tap water to her face, to hide any cheap and unwanted emotion that might pop up automatically in public.

She surveyed the room and saw that hell had broken lose. People were standing on their toes and wearing porcupine's heads. Their fingers were crossed at the edge of sanity, and their gripping knees were gradually losing their foundation. The jungle drum was beating louder; the captives' perspiration was pouring by the buckets. The ultimate climax could not be postponed, as mourners started to embrace one another.

'Did you hear how the reporter sung out the meaning of life?' Edwin cried. 'She tells her listeners how we must reflect on our lives. Life isn't an act of consuming everything that lies in our path. It's an art of living with others. We shouldn't use others as a means for something else, but as an end in itself. My grandpa has stirred all this in us. The principle of the soul ties the living and the dying together—people asking themselves how they want to be remembered. People are asking themselves what it means to have a soul. They want to know how many new friends they have made each day. Having friends is preferable to loneliness, and solitude. Friendship brings about trust and tolerance among people. Today my grandpa is transmitting a very important message—pause and rediscover yourself. And you'll find out that life isn't alienated from community.'

'You've a peculiar way to say that the announcer realizes how simple her life could have been. And were it not for Ralph, she would have continued to see her life as an abstraction.'

'Community soul inspires people how to live,' said Mr Cougar. 'The moral of this is that it does not interfere with whatever religion a person might have.'

'For my good deeds, you should be grateful. I could easily have removed your common sense,' the Timeman said. Neither Edwin nor Mr Cougar replied to their adversary. 'You've done a lot of talking about community soul. How does it interact with the body? Is it distinct from the body? Where does it harbor itself? You couldn't answer me, because there are only brain activities. And all mental activities are caused by brain activities. I preserve only the last conscious impression.'

'Picking out the ontological status of the soul is least important,' replied Mr Cougar. 'What it means to have a soul is the question. This question is best answered with respect to the nature of life. And the meaning of life is construed in terms of community soul—making friends and wanting to be remembered by others,' he said, hoping that the Timeman wouldn't press the issue further.

'Yes, we teach ourselves how to live. And we cultivate ourselves as though our lives were governed by the principle of the soul,' Edwin added.

'Edwin, why don't you talk about your true feelings?' the Timeman asked. Edwin glanced at his grandpa who nodded at him. He didn't really understand his grandpa's encouragement because the Timeman wanted to make them prisoners. Edwin waited for a brief moment and then began to speak:

'Timeman, there's a certain thing about dying you'll never be able to comprehend—loss and sorrow. My feeling of sorrow is like an abstraction to me. It's a very bitter loss. I see my own meaningless existence. My mother's face, my sister's, and father's—none can hide their pain. I can't help them. I can't be with them when they really need me. I don't think that my family deserves all this suffering. Their tortures have begun. And with each advancing second, their sadness intensifies.' He paused for a moment.

'Aren't you the one who sings out the glory of the community soul?'

'Yes, what I see before me is unbearable. When someone who I dearly care for and love is dying, a part of me also dies. The philosophy of soul and resurrection doesn't comfort my family or me. Losing a loved one would be like losing my right arm. My daily life would be affected without a limb. This is what my mind will lose, love.'

'Your grandpa is the one to be blamed for all of this. For a constellation, you'll learn about Ralph's deception at four o'clock.'

'For some reason I'm very angry with my grandpa. I feel like I hate him. He shouldn't do this to us. And yet, who am I to understand my grandpa's suffering, vanishing from his family and friends. It must be more terrible for him than us. We can speak about our sadness, but he couldn't. He is dying all alone as though he had never existed. Besides all this, my grandpa's death means much more than all our pain and sufferings combined together. He's noble in his quest. And I will defeat you because I love my grandpa.'

'You shouldn't have said so much about your feelings. It has a negative effect on your grandpa. It makes him see his own folly. Let's see some more about your grandpa's community,' suggested the Timeman.

14:15 National Solidarity and Condolence

Kiskinavapa, a well-known radio announcer from Radio Montreal with about thirty years of experience behind him, hesitantly got off his working chair, rubbing his face and eyes forcefully and paced the floor back and forth in his medium-sized studio. Out of habit, he knew that the sentimental hymn he had put on for his audience would not be finished yet, and he listened to the melody:

Go Home

I spread my wings for the glory land
I'm ready to be in your hand
O, I want to sleep in your kingdom
Take me away because I feel so down

Take me, take me, take me to my throne

To where everyone else has gone before
How beautiful the crimson sky plays off the shore
Reminding me how I long to be by your door
Look at me how I'm a crying soar

Take me, take me, take me home
I wanna go home
O, I wanna come home

The harvesting is coming to an end
The birds don't come around the bend
The wind is down
And I don't know how I would come around

Home, home, my home
I'm coming to my throne

I live so long and roam the world
Till now, I've never seen my soul
Where's my dome?
Don't stop me to go home

The rainbow calls out my name
Why don't I come home?
Take me, take me, take me to my throne

He lit a cigarette and took a few deep puffs one after the other. He looked like a child waiting for his mother to lead him by the arm. He could not figure out what was happening to him; his approaching retirement occurred to him. He stared at the transparent glass wall separating his office; nobody was in the opposite studio. Feeling the warm cigarette butt on his finger tips, he finally found his way back to his chair, which never failed to do its magical transformation in the worst situation. Putting his elbows on his table, he put his thumb in his mouth and waited for the song to finish.

He pulled the microphone closer to his lips and looked straight ahead, a look that could bypass any physical barrier, 'Oh, dearest Cougar! Look what you've done to us,' he cried mournfully and softly. In the next instant his mood flipped like a coin, as though he was angrily reading out everyone's sentiment. 'You want to slip out from the eternal flow of time. We should digest our overloaded raw feeling fully. We should stock up on intrinsic human relationships and mend the forgotten pride and dignity in our lives. Oh, yes. Tell me how much we'd like to balance out the past with the future. We're condemned to the frozen national solidarity brewing up around the country: from the East Coast to the West; from the North to the South, from the young to the old; from the weak to the strong; from occasional sightseers to permanent residents; and from theists to atheists. The entire country is stagnant like a barren land singing out its melancholy hymn in the cool winter. Yes, we're waiting like a sleeping ocean dreaming how the breeze should tickle our spineless back. Oh, we sit like a helpless fire drowning itself in its own sorrow.

'Our American friends bordering us, from Maine to Washington, couldn't quickly spit out our influence....' The announcer was hinting at the CBC radio station, which pushed its traditional non-commercial programs to refurnish a delicious taste for the elite in society—the educated. ' For sure, we have something to learn from all this. Cultural regression bounces off from Sandreef. An isolated community stretches its wings across nations. That's the old root that still lives in us like a sleeping mountain yawning its first breath to the deep blue sky. And its snowy peak pointing to a gigantic Sandreef in the middle of nowhere. Sandreef is a sandy shore glittering like a golden mushroom. Before it, all else humbles as weaklings. And yet, it *is* notorious for fading footprints of people who once passed by.

'Our soul miraculously escapes the rat race of everyday struggling. With that, we can snatch a glimpse of life's precious secrets. Look for ourselves how Sandreef is transforming— an entire nation and some American States to almost affectionate and receptive communities. Mr Cougar's Sandreef hides itself off the map and from people's traveling plans. Poor travelers, how you like to have something solid in your hands? You're curious enough to point your finger to Sandreef. Consult maps, telephone government offices, police stations – none of these can help you. These offices also rely on street maps. Why don't you settle for Rose Hall instead?' Kiskinavapa took a breath and then put on the song – *The Nameless*:

Look how you're dancing in the light.
Is your destiny holding out that bright?
Sing to us that you're right,

Wait, I'll give you some of my insight.

Nobody knows my name,
Am I crying out to you in vain?
But, I'll always be the same,
Believe in me even in the worst rain.

You're a little poor song nobody wants to sing,
You couldn't be hummed in the wind,
Your community washes you up and takes you in,
And I don't know what your grumbling will bring.

Are you like your mother who casts you out in clay?
She still tries to clean you by muddying you up for the next
day,
You're a poor song coming our way,
I'll tell your mom not to make you go astray.

As the news flew swiftly onward and consumed people off guard, most motorists traveling between cities stumbled onto local radio stations to hear the incredible story that was unfolding from direct and passionate reporters of the mystery man, Mr Cougar. The drama of his courage and sentiment became known as the mystery of life and death that could be explained in a wink.

Kiskinavapa shifted in his chair and cried out: 'Let's go to Vicky for a direct update on the traffic situation. Vicky! What's the present situation like?' She had been a well-known companion for motorists. During the worst snowstorm, she was out there with her helicopter crews to report road conditions.

'Thank you, Kiskinavapa,' she answered.

'What's happening on the roads, Vicky?' he repeated, hoping that she would be precise and brief.

'Yes, Kiskinavapa. Nearly all of the stations have abruptly interrupted their regular programs to accommodate the story of endless traffic jams throughout the country. You should see how human intrinsic values are pilling up at the roadside. I've never seen this before. It's a natural disaster on highways and local roads on this beautiful sunny day. Motorists are reducing their speed limit to less than a half of the maximum. Cars, trucks, vans, buses, and motorbikes are sitting at road corners and in emergency lanes without the slightest mechanical failures. It's like waiting for the sermon on the road to end.'

'You mean to say there isn't any explanation for all this, Vicky?'

'Kiskinavapa, these commuters believe that missing a sentiment would be considered high treason. Oh, yes, it'd be unforgivable. Some families with children are kicking pebbles on roads; senior residents have abandoned their coaches and formed repentance groups along dangerous highways. From up here, I can sense how people are sharing the feeling of how life could be quickly snatched away. Traffic in the city couldn't crawl any slower.'

'Thanks, Vicky,' he cried, acknowledging a colleague who stood on the same side of the fence as he did. 'No accidents, fog, rain, or road construction could impede driving conditions. And yet, air-conditioned vehicles have their windows fully open to allow the blue of life to come in. Yes, the blue – like a burning cigarette between a smoker's fingers. Back to you, Vicky!'

'Yes, Kiskinavapa. There isn't any hurrying on the road. Only the greed for information, the desire to detect every single word on the radio, the harmony of living with the meaning of what life really amounts to. All this renders drivers to some automatic functions – listening, driving, and speaking out with their headlights on. A driver in a red car, the one with a Vancouver license plate in the right lane, turns off his tape recorder on his lonely journey. He's amazed to encounter other motorists throwing about the virtue of patience on the road. Everybody driving with the windows fully open says it all. Hearts are crying out that life is precious. Most drivers politely glance at others to share the same feelings and sympathy, like a monotonous old tune without any blazing flame. To obey this unwritten code on the road seems innate like a revelation of how to be humble to oneself. Look there, a driver is taking in the glance from another driver! That tells the unforgettable story of how people should walk with respect and courtesy because they don't want to wake up with the beast in themselves. Kiskinavapa, it seems that the unconscious is playing its role in commuters' driving habits. It could only be that the fear of death has been awakened. Over to you, Kiskinavapa.'

Over the past few minutes, Kiskinavapa had been looking at a sheet of paper that a colleague had given him. He scanned it again with his hand and then turned off the automatic music machine that usually came on by itself after a second of silence.

He wondered where it would all stop and then reported, 'Our telephone company is joyfully crying out Christmas season telephoning; choking operators screech out work overload. Customers are tolerating a limited number of free lines without complaining. Being cut off abruptly, buzzing and hissing with interference: all this shows us that the virtue of our community is tolerable. The community in us flourishes when dying is the ultimate price. Cellular phone users on bicycles, in parks, on street corners, in buses and trains, on the Rocky mountains, in the woods, in rest-rooms—all of them are getting the news from friends and family members with a jungle of colors added to the message. Some family members are phoning their loved ones on the road, to reassure them how rare life is. The phone brings people together and gets the latest development to any remote situation. Some farmers working without radios wait on their family members to satisfy their unquenchable hunger, hunger that can't grow on the ground. Fanatics across the country are desperately trying to express their gratitude and solidarity to any residents in Sandreef. Are we feeling guilty? Guilty for what?' He waited for the music to come on automatically.

He interrupted the music and gave a brief introduction of the current situation to new listeners and then continued, 'The bonds among family members and friends are sprouting like weeds during the rainy season. The family is reincarnated from a grain of sand. All this Mr Cougar meant to us. This is the essential value to live by. Most private and public elderly homes around the country can't handle all the telephone calls from family members and friends. For death, love and despair—

common as they appear to all—belong only to the living. Some adults are consulting their high school graduation books to pick up misplaced pieces from friends and colleagues; some marriages with freely-swinging hatchets are being saved.

'Teenagers and young adults are forming equal partnerships with their parents and peers in this ultimate moment of communal living. Solidarity without believers could not tie us together. But don't forget, the nightmare for ambulances, fire fighters, and police—none of them could work freely like our mourners. Severe medical cases have had to be flown to hospitals by helicopter. Let's check in with the traffic. Vicky, are you with us?'

'Of course! As things look, an accident on any road would definitely turn out to be disastrous for the victim.'

Kiskinavapa quickly cut her off and then stared once more at the sheet before him. 'The family is reincarnated. Love and caring are back into life. We may wonder whether this is a genuine path toward the essence of community. Young adults are looking inwards. Our self-center types are reassessing their oversize personal achievements. Ordinary workers like myself are planning to spend more time with their families. Careless self-abusers are revising their personal habits.

'We hear the call for health, and it is overshadowing people's eating habits. More recreation and sufficient sleep would alter the nature of work drastically, tomorrow. People are searching for ways to participate in more social activities; this will be the new standard of living. Families are planning more vacations and hoping to enjoy health to its fullest extent. All this does not only speak out against our superficial values, a contagious disease, trying to wipe out every living thing on the planet, but sings out a new life, not for the reinvention of the wheel, but for just cleaning its spokes once in a while.' He slowly uttered the last four words and waited for the song, *A Lonely Mountain,* to come on:

You're sitting like a mountain
Looking at the river goes by

O your head touching the clouds
But you couldn't fly

Don't think about yourself as being so gray
And you're swimming in your tear
Angels don't have to hear your cry
To tell you that not to be a pain in the sky

Don't be a spectator of life
Come down to the meadow
For a big bite
O it'd make you feel so high

Don't cloudy up your smile
For it's how you honor life
Don't be a river of sadness
For a lonely mountain couldn't hide

Radios teach listeners of their inherent abilities to mystify images from lose words. And yet, some impatient listeners hopped from one station to another for the most passionate talk shows. And reporters, in turn, haunted the streets for local prey with the shrewdest opinions to satisfy their faithful audiences. As the radio also reduced listeners to the herd, the slight breeze that was blowing across the country confronted no significant resistance, and it opened some closed minds.

To satisfy people's creative imaginations, some radio stations quickly dragged in guest speakers, mostly professionals and celebrities. Some mayors and provincial and federal politicians attempted to put some rhetoric into a single person who powerlessly held Canadians in the palm of his hand.

'Everybody wants to know who Mr Cougar is!' Kiskinavapa raised his voice. 'His true identity. All these intriguing questions without any answers make journalists seem like gravediggers. Some are looking for his bank records, his place of birth, a criminal record, a group affiliation, and his parents' history. Why don't they look for his religious balance sheet, too? On the other side of the fence, do we have a simple man who wants to die?

'Does anyone have an identity with Mr Cougar's situation? By the grace of God, nobody has committed suicide yet. Hospitals and psychiatric clinics forecast the bitter possibilities of death, accidents, injuries, and suicide. All this could happen, regardless of the outcome of Mr Cougar! Medical staff and the police are preparing themselves.

'Mr Cougar is becoming much more than a mysterious figure for us,' he remarked sarcastically. 'Some local residents speak about him as being an extremely holy man. Let's listen to their views: "Mr Cougar never kills an ant or a cockroach. He lives like in the Biblical era, with fish. He reminds me of the apostle Peter. I tell you, he can see into the future." Here is another local resident on the line: "He's a true healer. Once Mr Cougar rubbed my back, and after that, I never had any back pain again." Here, we've another resident: "Mr Cougar is merciful! He's our spiritual leader, a harmless servant of God. And he knows the secret of life."

'Not everyone shares the same opinion about Mr Cougar; there is also the jealous and malevolent side. Let's hear this local resident: "He's a king of the sharks! And always swimming with those man-eating monsters." Another resident expressed an altogether different view of the mystery man: " That Cougar is a dirty alien from some distance stars. His spaceship sank in the ocean. Eyewitnesses saw it that night. But he's the only survivor. He wants to enslave us. For sure, he had to be an alien. Look for yourself how he's burning himself out. He needs water to survive. And before that, he had problems showing his age. He never had a wrinkle or a gray hair before. He can't be human. Look at him. He doesn't even age like us. And he's drinking up water just like a fish. We couldn't do this or else we'd be blown up like a balloon and explode. If we aged like him, smoke would pour out from our ears…. I tell you, one day he just popped up here, just like that. He just took the form of a young man. He isn't one of us."

'Do you believe this speaker, that Mr Cougar can't age like us— like normal people? Obviously, some members of his community also hate the unexplained.'

Insinuating that he was an alien drove fear and curiosity, friendliness and resentment, simplicity and advancement, ignorance and knowledge, regret and confinement, and guilt and praise into some people. Space watchers thought that they would have hard evidence for the alien hypothesis. They were busy checking their data with astronomers for any unusual sign or event in the 1940s on the Northeast coast of Newfoundland. But even if he was really a creature from out of space, people had, and were accepting him like their own, flesh and blood.

'The call,' said Edwin.

'What do you mean by that?' asked the Timeman.

'Kiskinavapa is a caller. He's waking up the community within people. And people are responding. It is unbearable to die without knowing that we have a soul. People are becoming aware of themselves. They start to recognize the meaning of having a soul.'

'No, they're lessening the intensity of the unknown.'

'Yes, death is seen as a taboo. My grandpa believes that the afterlife is also honorable. This is what he is saying to everybody. People will identify themselves with the honor of living with each other. This is a positive value in a society and among different cultures.'

'Ralph is cultivating worshipers!'

'No, nobody worships my grandpa's soul or him. His way of life is an example for others. His community soul is needed nowadays, because living on the same street doesn't hold neighbors together.'

'And how is that?'

'Mythologies provide answers to most unexplained events in human life. People used to ask themselves about the afterlife. Was that all in life? High priests invented supernatural beings to not only control and suppress people, but also to reward followers. People believed in an afterlife that was rewarded lavishly by gods and goddesses. Mythologies had a function—they united people.

'Religions replace mythologies. People still believe in the existence of the soul, God, and so on. Religions give up answers about death, re-incarnation, and soul.

'Today, people alienate themselves from the essence of life. Sciences force us to believe in only physical things. There aren't any souls or re-incarnation. We are becoming ultra individualistic. We see our neighbors as unfriendly and untrustworthy. We live like spies. We can't continue to live like this. My grandpa brings hope to us.

'Kiskinavapa hasn't created any new values for listeners. He has merely expressed what is within people. It seems to me that people see themselves differently. They want to work on how they should be remembered in society. All this means much more than money to us. The announcer spoke about his inner feelings. He noticed that my grandpa had reminded him about his soul.'

'The soul isn't an extra entity. But it is like an image which reflects a person's entire life in society.'

'Yes,' said Edwin, waiting for the Timeman to take them to some other events.

14:30 The Hymn

Reporters and radio announcers were surpassing their journalistic skills. With their brilliance, exacerbated with twilight intelligence and sentiment, they encompassed their faithful listeners. Hymns and gospel music mingling with frequent intermittence hypnotized their devoted audiences, as the beloved patient's physical condition glowed on the horizon. In a Vancouver radio station, Corrine Harding, a young broadcaster with a flair for details, sang with her omnipresent abilities. Like most stations searching for diversity, a dosage of public opinions was heard and contrasted with scholarly arguments. Medical doctors talked freely of their benevolent professional experiences regarding the normal aging process of human beings. The most notorious prediction of people's behavior came from psychologists. Besides all these intriguing inquires, Corrine Harding's show was quite popular, and she was broadcasting an interview she had made fifteen minutes ago.

'Oh, in our airports, there are uncountable faces yawning while some murmur about Mr Cougar. Yonder, an old man is walking around with a dried and wrinkled face,' Corrine said. 'A mountaineer; we need to tackle a face like that. If a climber loses his grip, we'd say those corn-flake-like skins on his face are just too big for him. What a sad case that poor old man is. Since when has he had an interest in life or death. Were he lying on a deserted street for a snooze, he'd look too stale for the morgue. He still moves; and yet, no life can be seen within him.

'Life, where is your vitality? Is it only in young adults? How charming! Some of them are leaning against a huge glass window

98

not so far from me. They've carved themselves in strength and courage. I see it all. A jet could easily fly between the vertical lines on their forehead. Farmers could use them for irrigation in the rainy season.

'Next to the ploughed foreheads, others are looking up in the sky. What manner of hollowness bounces off their reflective minds? Oh, they're the wondering types having their mouths half open on their blank faces. Walls like these were abolished in office buildings. Could it be that depression and creativity wear the same look? At least these inventive mourners wait for the light to flash in them—eureka! Oh, I might as well run away from this dream world. It's too risky and contagious. It could capsize the little boat that holds my sanity.

'Am I seeing right? Only fifty meters away, a woman is trotting with her luggage. She rechecks the sign overhead "Departure Building." Look, she doesn't have enough time to smile. Her four-year-old daughter has a runny nose and struggles to keep up with her. Her little hand grabs her mother's skirt. The woman stops and looks about for dreadful line-ups, and now the child has a chance to wipe her nose on her mother's skirt. Luckily I've a strong stomach.

'The woman thought of herself as being late. Check-in clerks give her strange looks. How could this passenger learn about her fear of flying? She only thinks about catching her plane and arriving home on time. Surprisingly, she looks around for other passengers. I bet she'll join the crowd near the screen. She remembers her little girl and takes her firmly by the hand. The woman looks a bit nervous and perplexed, as she hesitantly walks toward the crowd. Just as the story of tragedy has been told, there's always a storyteller on the scene. The newcomer is listening attentively to how Mr Cougar's dying plays on her fear of flying.

'Let's go and speak to one of those check-in clerks. They must be bored in this saga. The middle-aged woman, right next to the young man, seems to have a lot of experience under her sleeves. Her intelligence dazzles in her sparkling eyes. Hello, don't passengers want to board their planes anymore?'

'Well, well! If I must say, our passengers are talking about how they don't want to fly right now.' the clerk joyfully cried.

'Are you not terribly sad because Mr Cougar will die?' asked Corrine.

'It's just like flying. Your life is in someone else's hands.'

'Madam, we aren't talking about flying, but dying!'

'Yes, people aren't passive passengers. Oh, no. They heartily and sincerely participate in reaching their destination safely. At no time is a passenger a quitter. He never loses hope.'

'What hope?'

'The hope to reach home safe and sound.'

'A miserable loser that Cougar is, wouldn't you say so?'

'How can anybody say that? Hope is the answer. Hope until the engine is turned off. On a flight, passengers started something. They wanted to see the end. Yes, the end it had to be. They kept themselves wined-up to the last second. A flight has to come to an end. And there's no other way.'

'So, Mr Cougar was one of your passengers? Isn't this what you're saying?'

'No, no! We're travelers. Our belts are tightened up, and they won't come lose until the goal that was conceived is reached. When we arrive at our destination, there's no winner to boast about his ravishing and cherished prize.'

'If I can get you straight, human destiny can't be any different than the desire to turn the last stone. We've trained ourselves to see everything after life as real,' Corrine commented and then hesitated to move away from her. 'Specialists predict a catastrophe, a real disaster at ever airport. I haven't seen any disaster. Only passengers who are forming little groups all over the corridor and not boarding their planes.'

' When pilots are on strike, all planes are grounded, too. There's no problem. Planes don't fly without passengers. It's that simple.'

'So, you don't expect any accidents, loss of lives, do you?'

'Like other airports, we're informed that everything will be back to normal after four o'clock. The bulletin went out internationally. Some incoming flights have been detoured to the US for a while. Our airport is more or less crowded. As you can see, there aren't any hassles or emergencies here.'

'Why are you so calm and self-confident as though this is an ordinary day?'

'I used to be a flight attendant, but I'm too old for it now.'

'Yes, I see. That work had to be very nerve-wracking!'

'No. Not the work, it was phenomenal. But zooming through different time zones was the killer. Just going to Europe, you jump about eight hours into the future, from evening to midday. Right here, we have time differences. In spring we jump one hour back and in the fall, one hour then forward. And that's nothing, isn't it? Today at four, we'll just restart the clock. Come to think about it, this Cougar fellow, he makes a lot of sense. We should have four working shifts: The evening one from four to ten; the night one from ten to four; the morning one from four to ten; and the midday one from ten to four.'

'This is interesting. Are you sympathetic to Mr Cougar's forthcoming death?'

'Well, just like everybody else. I still think there's a meaning to it. But I just can't put my finger on it....'

'Thank you for your insight, and goodbye!' cried Corrine. 'It's not hectic here. Passengers and family members are refreshing their relationships. It's just a wonderful family occasion. Now, we should break away for some commercials.' She saw a gripping union sweep across the country; she looked down at her feet for a solid and stable surface under them. She imagined a windmill anchored to the ground. And Mr Cougar was the wind. The windmill cried out to the wind to stop blowing. She slipped to another stream of consciousness: she entertained some images of coastal water.

She imagined that ships were deliberately entering the Canadian waters and that none were leaving. She entertained enriched images of the Pacific and Atlantic coasts. Suddenly, she asked her colleague, who was sitting opposite her to get a tape about tidal waves and ships' engines. She tested it and then left it on the radio as the background. She believed that human beings had a sailing instinct.

'Where are all the waves now gone? They were sunk under.

Hundreds of ships had buried them down to the ocean bed. No waves are hugging the coastline. Cargo ships and cruisers are making all sizes of funnels in the ocean. Oh, our oceans are crying out in dismay, for too many tornadoes are drilling themselves to the ocean bed. And yet, no conceivable harm is in sight. This would be the last thing any crew would want to see.

'Ships that are supposed to leave the harbor as scheduled, linger around without causing any suspicion. In the name of security and safety, the logs are rechecked. Some stay out of range to keep their radio lines open. The oceans are idle with its cargo, holding back the tide of human displacement. A friendly coastal blockade of Canada goes by without any notice. Not one crew complains. In due course, all things have to come to an end.

Sailors sing out that Mr Cougar must have his destiny. Like members of a school of herrings, sailors swim around their short wave radios. Their best line is thrown out to capture a clear transmission. Their face tells the story of a lifetime experience waiting within arms' reach. Today, they stand as witnesses of how a person set out to master death. Mr Cougar couldn't be left unheard and unattended,' she said and then took a pause.

'Mr Cougar teases an appetite in us. I can't move my feet away from it. It awakens my fear of not fully having had an enjoyable life yet. Doesn't this turn out to be an impenetrable barrier for us? Life cannot go on without any notice, as the world waits for Mr Cougar who neither detests death nor cherishes all the virtues life had to still offer him. Now, he lives out my life in slow motion while he turns over the last stone to see its ultimate truth.

'And yet, my children cannot fully comprehend my emotions. I try to show them the importance of life. And that angels fly around with wings. I tell them what dying meant among angels. My children resist it all. They haven't lived long enough, and they don't want to join the angels. When I look inward, I see myself as an endless - risk-taker. Do life and death amount to the loss of loving and the fear of being left alone without it? I think about myself as though I'll live forever. This means for me that my love for life has never been lost, but it was just misplaced somewhere. Mr Cougar's coming death has awakened up a natural precaution in me. From now on, I won't miss out from my goodness because it belongs to the living.

'Neither laws nor dictatorship, nor totalitarianism government could make me a disloyal participant of the Mr Cougar's way. He shows me self-unity without nationalism, and that could sleep in my bed without evoking any quarrel as to whose turn is it to turn off the light.'

'Grandpa, don't you want to say anything?' asked Edwin, realizing that he often tried to enter into their conversation impolitely.

'No, my child. Pure reason in itself makes me just half of a person. Before I react, reality has changed. I can't be as natural as you are. I'm sorry my child,' he replied, appearing to be tired because he was still affected by Edwin's revelation of hate and frustration.

'Airports and oceans, the announcer spoke allegorically and metaphorically about how we are travelers. She was saying that life is a journey, with starting and ending points. At birth it began. And every little step of accomplishment leads to goals. We shouldn't lose sight of the final goal. If we bring the final goal of life to the forefront, then friendship, respect, trust, equality, and freedom would enrich the quality of our life in society. Yes, the traveler and the search for something intangible to live for. My grandpa has offered us community soul.'

'Are you saying that the meaning of the soul today is the community soul? And the afterlife depends on whether or not you're remembered by your community? How bemused I am.'

'Not exactly,' Edwin challenged. 'Life is like a leaf in a flowing stream. As the water undergoes perpetual changes around the leaf, the leaf still retains its identity. The water is like events and happenings around our lives. Mind you, I'm not saying that we don't act and react on situations. The essence of life is the community soul in us.

'I am thinking about some murderous dictators in our history. We remember their gruesome acts as inhumane. Society helps us to remember people who were responsible for awesome atrocities as a means to prevent other such acts from happening.

'The principle of community soul defeats selfishness, boredom, loneliness, and individualism. At the airport, we saw lonely people waiting for deliverance. The sailor is a symbol for searching. And sailing in a circle is about coming home empty handed. The traveler—it doesn't matter where he goes—takes his community soul with him.'

'Keep your enthusiasm riding. You'll really need it when we visit the next series of events,' he instructed. Edwin was ready, but Mr Cougar appeared to be miserable.

14:45 Is Cougarism Possible?

From a single seed in Sandreef a flower blossomed in the sunlight, pollinating into everyone's home and abolishing personal privacy. It gripped home-dwellers like a hypnotic spell; it ran through cats and dogs: all of them stared at the television. They waited for the tragic story of death to come to an end. The CBC, being one of the most popular national TV stations in Canada, had been conducting a live close-up interview in the streets. The broadcasting started about twenty-five minutes ago. But a few minutes ago, John Blackman, the commentator who was an ordinary household name, witty, spontaneous, a middle-aged reporter, came to the scene. Viewers knew his round-table discussion would put everything in order. And he would hold the nation by its toes. The bottom part of the television screen had been showing images from City TV: Mr Cougar and his room, his temperature, his heartbeat, and pulse rate. On the upper part of the screen, the announcer sat at a round table as though he was waiting for his guests. But his six guests were sitting in different CBC studios across the country. With modern camera tricks, viewers had the impression that everyone was sitting in the same studio around the same table.

'We're here to unravel whether Cougar is possible,' he cried. 'From you out there, we truly want to know how you feel. Do you believe that Mr Cougar could die? Let's go to our first guest, doctor Steiner.' Dr Steiner's image appeared on the right of the announcer as though he was sitting next to him, and not at a CBC station in British Columbia. He was popular with lay people for explaining medical techniques. 'Doctor Steiner, can anybody will his own death?

Do you think Mr Cougar will die at four this afternoon?'

'Medically speaking, until now, we know that we can't will our own deaths anymore than we can will the growth of a tooth. All this is pure nonsense! In my opinion, mind you, this Cougar fellow is scandalous. He should be jailed,' he replied confidently as though he wanted his listeners to be more attentive.

'Can you give us a straight scientific assessment of Mr Cougar's health, Doctor Steiner?'

'From his vital signs, everything seems to be normal to me. I would need some tests before making a diagnosis. As it seems from here, he looks normal and healthy. Mind you, doctors aren't into the business of predicting when somebody will die. To put it bluntly, our job is to save life, not stop it. Medically, we know when someone is near death. But again, we can't say exactly when. This Cougar case is completely outrageous. He should be committed and locked up in a psychiatric clinic. Perhaps, this man escaped from a clinic.'

'Here, you have Doctor Steiner's scientific opinion. But Doctor, how could you explain his normal vital signs? They don't correspond with his aging process. About one year every fifteen minutes. Is this normal?'

'It's intriguing, isn't it? His kidneys must be overworking. I must confess, it's like a conspiracy against medicine. He doesn't even urinate. He should already look like a hippo. But medically, this man can't will his own death. Maybe he's suffering from some rare disease.'

'Ralph, if that doctor cuts you up, he won't find a soul or mind in your body. Don't you agree?' asked the Timeman. Mr Cougar did not reply.

'If you're saying that my grandpa is making a false personal knowledge claim about his coming death, I disagree,' Edwin replied to the Timeman. 'My grandpa doesn't have to justify what he directly knows about himself. The mere fact that he is conscious of himself makes his claim self-evident. Yes, my grandpa wouldn't be mistaken about his own death. He has direct access to his body. Let's get it straight, everybody knows the difference between having a headache from a toothache.

'Life must be cultivated. And whatever remains after death is what we call the soul—community soul. Our sciences reveal a lot of facts about man. But parapsychology investigates our phenomenal abilities—telepathy, astro-projection, and so on. These powers of the mind appear to be linked to our spiritual side. Perhaps, my grandpa foresaw his future.'

'Are you saying that your grandpa has a spiritual aspect?' interrupted the Timeman. 'This is pure nonsense.'

Mr Cougar broke his silence: 'For over nine years, I've been waiting for this day. And it has finally arrived. If I had known more about my past, I could have been able to reveal the source of my knowledge. Unfortunately, my friend, Lewis, knows more about me than I do.' The silence didn't last long until other events popped up.

'Thank you, Doctor Steiner. Ms Merville is also our guest today.' She appeared to have a seat next to the doctor. 'Ms Merville, do you think this Cougar fellow is going to die today?'

'We're cosmic beings,' Ms Merville, a well known astrologer from Montreal, replied sternly. She had predicted Perrie Elliot Trudeau's divorce, the great flood in Quebec that killed thousands of caribou, a tragic accident killing a famous British person, and still the last major war on earth occurring in twenty-twenty-three. 'Mr Cougar is very receptive to his own cosmic energy in the universe. He sees his own faith. And everything is tailored to fit for him. Can't you see that he doesn't need a doctor to treat what comes naturally? We can't put life in a pigeonholes like our doctor here. There's much more to humans than text book medicine.'

'In other words, Ms Merville, you're saying he'll pass away,' insisted the announcer.

'Yes, but his radiance will live for a long time to come. Everybody has a unique aroma. And that's why a dog, for example, could sniff it out.'

'Ms Merville, are you saying he'd definitely die at four?'

'Of course.'

'Do you've any evidence, Ms Merville?'

'Not rocks and stones from which you could trip and break your neck. His word is sufficient for me.' She hesitated for a few seconds, as though she was staring at a blank wall in front of her. 'To tell you the truth, I'm broken hearted. I'm worried about him. My whole body shivers with fear. I feel so weak and helpless in losing him. I don't know how to tell you my feelings. I feel a deep love for Mr Cougar. If there was anything I could do for him,' her voice shook. Some viewers were left weeping after her honest revelation.

The announcer struggled to hide his sentiment, as he wiped his face with his hand, and then spoke louder in a rough voice, 'You didn't foresee his death, I guess?'

With tears on her eyes, she could not control her pounding heart. 'No,' she murmured in a feeble voice.

'Ralph, this sounds much more like the truth about you. Do you believe that you have mystic qualities?' asked the Timeman.

'I don't have seven senses,' answered Mr Cougar. 'But after what you have done to me, with my consciousness and my body, I should believe that I am a mystical being.'

'There isn't any harm in believing in astrology. Beliefs don't hurt anybody,' Edwin cried. 'I don't think that it is important to enquire how he knows about his coming death.'

'Let me show you some other beliefs about life, soul, and death. Observe well!' the Timeman said to Edwin and Mr Cougar.

'Father August, What do you think about all this? Do you think he'll die today?' the announcer asked hoarsely.

The Catholic priest was happy to be interviewed, as he smiled cheerfully into the camera. He appeared to be sitting on the right of Ms Merville. 'It's unbearable to hear all these anti-Christian things about death. Nobody, not even Mr Cougar could will his own death. Death, I say to you, is God's business. When He's ready for you, you can't escape. God doesn't tell anybody when his time is up. And nobody, I repeat—nobody, knows God's mind. And don't let anybody tell you otherwise. God wills death. May God forgive us, I pray.' He stared into the camera again.

'I see,' cried Blackman. 'Couldn't it be that someone else from above told Mr Cougar about his death?'

'That's possible. But remember, Cougar is a true Christian, not an atheist. Everybody is talking about how he practiced love, kindness, and brotherhood to his fellow man.' The priest reminded the audience of the many empty churches these days.

'Perhaps, he's a saint!' the commentator cried.

'Well, this isn't for me to decide. But he's dying in a true Christian fashion. Look at how he's smiling. He has no fear of death, and he's waiting for God to open His arms for him.'

'Thank you, Father August, for your enlightened view.' The speaker said before he had a full-blown sermon on his show.

'Ralph,' interrupted the Timeman, 'at four o'clock they should turn the body right to go to heaven. And left to go to hell.'

'Lying on my back is Ok. We need much more than food to live. Our nourishments come from several sources. Some of us need religious beliefs. Some still want material objects. Some want both. We have atheists among us too. It is healthy to add some spiritual ingredients to our food. Community soul is about how to live a dignified and respectful life,' answered Mr Cougar.

'Yes, Timeman. Maybe God told him that he would die today,' Edwin added.

'Ralph, why do you believe that you will pass away at four?'

'I thought that I had known it all along. But, after hearing you, nothing is for sure anymore. I don't know how all this will really end.'

'This is much more interesting for me,' said the Timeman. Edwin wanted to say something but he held back. 'Ralph, you evoke fear in your community, the fear of death. When all this is over, your community will know that the domain of death is still a barrier for human beings.'

'No, my grandpa isn't trying to conquer death. He is saying that we should conduct life in accordance with community soul. He tells us how to live. And how he wants his community to remember him. Death, for my grandpa, means reaching a point in which a person couldn't do anything more to improve himself in his community.'

'Are you telling me that community soul is a philosophy, a socio-moral one, which includes aspects of the philosophy of mind, body, and death?'

'What sort of treachery are you practicing on us?' asked Edwin. 'You're trying to confuse us. Let's get it straight. You have only one ambition—to abolish us in your time cell. What you said might be true. And yet, life, soul, and death are very important for everybody. By recognizing the fact that we live in a community, death becomes manageable for us. What comes first is that we should try to cultivate a positive community soul. After that, God's rewards or consequences follow. Community soul compliments religions.'

'Ralph, who are you?'

'From what I've known about myself, I've tried to live morally. My community contributes to my self-identity. And community soul is the seed of morality in society.'

'How do you want to be remembered?'

'I'm not an inventor of anything new. I'm just objectifying what my community has to offer.'

'Very modest. But you're still ignorant of your own nature. Learn some more about yourself, Ralph.'

The interview continued.

'Mind you,' interrupted Dr Steiner, 'in certain cases, we could tell whether a patient would die in an hour or so, not the exact time. From some accident cases, we can hear the dying bell ringing. And we can tell whether a patient will die in a few minutes or so. So we could predict a patient's death. Don't get me wrong. We try to make everybody live forever with everlasting health. And dying naturally isn't very interesting for us.'

The announcer accepted Doctor Steiner's viewpoint. He quickly introduced his next guest: 'Mr Fowler, it's good to have you on our show. How do you see all this?'

'I'm pleased to be here, Mr Blackman. Doctor Steiner, permit me, please. When are you going to die? I'm sure it's one of the most absurd questions you've ever been asked, haven't you? I figure, you can't answer me,' said Mr Fowler, one of the most expensive lawyers in Canada, specializing in criminal laws. He had defended some of the most gruesome criminals and Mafia bosses. Most of them belonged to the elite class of society. 'No test could tell you when? Am I not right? We just don't need any medical advice here, especially when dying occurs naturally. Am I right?'

'I see your point, Mr Fowler,' answered Doctor Steiner. 'We're not in the habit of walking in the street and telling passersby when they'd die. For me, Mr Cougar is a clown.'

'But Doctor! His aging, is that normal?'

'Once again, sir. We practice science, not guesswork. We work with patients, their medical records, their past and current conditions. As you know, hairdressers are into making people look eternally charming and beautiful, not me. On the medical side, a few children are born with rare genetic disorders called progeria or Hutchinson-Gilford syndrome. These children age about eight times faster than a normal child. And their life expectancy is about fifteen years after birth. But Mr Cougar, an adult, is aging about one year every fifteen minutes. So in a year, he should age over thirty-five thousand years compared with a normal person. So, we need evidence.'

'Well, Doctor, I disagree.'

'How odd would it be if I said, "hi George, I'm going to die today at four." You'd call a psychiatric wagon to come and get me. For sure, you'd think I was insane. But you don't know at the time that I'm pulling a hoax on you. Look at him, his vital signs are stronger than mine.' Everyone stared at the bottom section of the screen. The commentator quickly intervened before their dispute deteriorated any further.

'We've a well-known psychiatrist, Dr Markus from the Allen Memorial Hospital in Winnipeg in our studio now. Doctor, would you consider Mr Cougar a sane person? Or, is he like one of your patients at the clinic?'

'It's a million-dollar question you're asking me. More than half of the country is waiting for Mr Cougar. And another twenty thousands of them sit and wait in Sandreef for the ultimate outcome. To put it straight, if one of my patients told me that he'd die tomorrow, I'd make sure he was closely supervised, around the clock. For sure, Mr Cougar could die, if he has a chance to commit suicide. Like most everyone here, I'm suspicious of his motive. And we're waiting to see how he'll commit suicide—a gun or something. Another scenario—he might have poisoned himself several hours ago.'

'Are you saying that Mr Cougar is insane, dangerous to his own health? We should check under his bed. Perhaps, we would find something?'

'No, no! Most clinical cases are dealt with in that manner. Let see what he's done to us: He reinforces passengers' natural fear of flying, causing traffic jams all over the place. People want to get to the end of this matter. We want to know whether he can do it or not. Nobody wants to be left hanging. Not only this, we're participating in his ceremonial activity. Living it out, as though death is lying around the corner for each one of us.'

'Didn't he show us to be humble toward others?'

'Oh yes, this is positive. Another thing, the Hollywood way of life is coming to us, the idols for self-identification. We've our hero now, so we could model ourselves after him.'

'Isn't this an extraordinary event in human history – conquering death, Doctor Markus?'

'It surely gives us a cold shower. All of our lives we bitterly struggle to avoid the dying bed, but now it comes. It brings compassion, understanding, tolerance, family-togetherness, and enjoyment of the little we have.'

'Doctor Markus, what is Cougar's motive for announcing his own death four hours in advance?'

'Commanding death is absurd. This man doesn't sound like a dying person. It's more like a confused person, I'd say. His joy of dying is others' fear. One thing for sure, he really grips the entire nation on its toes,' replied the psychiatrist.

'Yes, it seems as if we can't understand all this anymore than any other lay person,' remarked the announcer.

The priest felt he had a duty to all Christian listeners: 'Life and death is in God's hands. If the Almighty wants him to die at four, he'll die. And nobody can stop that.'

'Let us go to Professor Barney, a prominent astronomer from the University of Toronto, who is sitting here beside me. Some people say that Mr Cougar is an alien. Do you have any record of a spaceship crashing off the coast of Halifax? Do you believe he's an alien?'

'All this is happening, too quickly,' Barney said. Nobody has had sufficient time to check all the records. I've been following the news since it came out. Some of my colleagues are checking past records for any unusual phenomena. Not only are we checking, but the CIA and the RCMP are into it much more than we are. They believe that Mr Cougar is a spy. Most importantly, they're trying to establish his identity. All we know, so far, is that he could be a foreign spy, but not an alien. Everybody is interested in him.'

'A spy, it's a big joke!" commented the announcer. There's only fish in Sandreef, and old run-down fishing boats. You can't be serious?'

'Yes, the RCMP and CIA are checking all sources: medical, dental, bank, criminal, and credit rating. I heard that his medical and bank record had disappeared. As you can see, there're many hands in this matter. Perhaps some foreign agents got to it before we did.'

'We're aware that your research is supported by the government. And you see things their way. Anybody could have stolen Mr Cougar's records because the price for them must be very high. Or, the RCMP wants to create a Canadian hero, so they've hidden his files. Anyway, do you think Mr Cougar is telling the truth?' challenged the announcer.

Smiling, and putting his arm on his chin, Barney continued, 'You ask for my judgment. Well, the universe is full of mysteries. The further into the past we look, the closer to the present we get. Even further back into the past, we can see the future. Everything is possible. If he decides to kick the bucket at four, that's fine with me. I've no objection. But can he really do it? It would definitely take more than a human being to do it.'

'Why do you think he can't do it?'

'We've seen that he's been aging extremely rapidly, but his internal organs hadn't undergone any changes whatsoever. Besides all this, life and death still remain a mystery, and I hope they still stay as such. We still can't see anybody's destiny on a star. It's a figure of speech. Don't get me wrong! I really don't know if each of us has a private star to hide in. And if Mr Cougar has found his, then that's good for him.'

'You've heard some opinions from our experts concerning Mr Cougar commanding death. Now, let us hear your view,' requested the announcer, as a list of toll free numbers flashed on the screen for callers.

'Don't get the outside to fool you,' said Ms Merville, 'telepathy, clairvoyance, precognition, are all well known today. How could you disregard cases such as, the old woman who lifted an entire car to save her grandchild? A woman ran back into a burning inferno to save her sleeping children. Look how he ages faster than Salomon O' Grandy—born on Monday and buried on Sunday.'

'Doctor Steiner, is it normal to age like this?' insisted the commentator.

'Without a comprehensive medical examination, I can't say anymore,' he answered, and he continued a professional posture.

'But doctor, from his physical appearances—hair and skin—one can see how he ages rapidly. Don't you agree?'

'Yes, there're noticeable changes. But don't get me wrong. Earlier, I heard that he had received some brain damage when he almost drowned. And he sometimes slips into short epileptic seizures. This patient belongs in hospital. And I insist that he should be taken to one. Look at him now, it's unbelievable that he's the same person I saw a while ago.'

'Doctor Steiner,' interrupted the lawyer, 'Removing Mr Cougar from his house without his authorization isn't advisable. Do it, if you really want to go to court. That's only the long-term consequence. The immediate one is how you'd pass those twenty thousand people near him.'

'Excuse me, I didn't mean it that way. This patient is an intriguing case study. A medical diagnosis is important. Well, I guess an autopsy would answer all our questions later.'

'Doctor, I don't think you've fully understood what I said. Mr Cougar has right and integrity. Be careful of making any scandalous remarks about my client being poisoned. Mr Cougar is dying a natural Christian death. Mind you, there won't be any autopsy either. It's Mr Cougar's last wish. The entire nation wants my client's image to be intact. There isn't any sound reason for thinking of foul play. Medical people see everything decent as a little experimental rat. It's something to chop up and put under a microscope. I assure you, Doctor Steiner, this gentleman is normal and conscious. And most of all, he isn't poisoned. And he isn't drugged. By all means, we can see that he isn't insane, Doctor.' Then the lawyer added that he would be Mr Cougar's family defense attorney free of charge. Mr Fowler had made himself clear in public, and he knew that most listeners sympathized with the patient.

'Yes, he's aging remarkably fast! With God, everything is possible,' cried the priest.

The announcer had allowed his guests to express their opinion freely: 'Who is Mr Cougar? We don't know anything concrete about him? We don't even know whether or not he's a religious person. Now let us go directly to our first caller. Hello, you're on the air.'

From the voice, one could easily tell it was an old woman on the phone. 'Everybody knows who Mr Cougar is. He has rights. I don't care if he's an alien or not. He's flesh-and-blood. A good man, with Canadian rights. And I'm proud to be a Canadian like Mr Cougar!'

'Yes, madam. You're absolutely correct. I don't think anybody wants to deport him. Not now, at least. All we want to clear up is why he has made a promise to us. And whether he's morally obligated to up hold his promise,' said the commentator, trying to be cleat about the discussion.

'I'm sure he's a good man. God forgives him. I've already offered up a prayer for him,' cried the priest, believing that God could comfort that poor woman had she gone to church.

'Dying is much more than a scientific or legal act,' interrupted Dr Markus, 'over twenty-seven million people are tearing their hearts out at this moment, regardless of the consequence. It's very sad to speak and feel this way about a person who enters into our life suddenly. We've a personal relationship with Mr Cougar. We should speak about him with decency. Everybody believes in him. Nothing can stop the clock now. Look at us. We can't even speak seriously about this poor man anymore. You want to know why? It's because we're trapped inside ourselves with an incomprehensible fear. We're talking about the fear of death. It's not a footprint on the shore which disappears with the tide.'

'Though that's quite observant of you,' cried the announcer. 'Everyday people are born and people die. Nobody ever makes any fuss about it. We go through our everyday lives as though nothing happens. Why should we kick up so much dust? But again, Mr Cougar's dying is very unique to us, especially the way he is going about it. Dying is much more than a game. We can't see what happens to us in its domain. What is the meaning of his dying? Is he really dying? With all respect and condolence, Mr Cougar is only saying he's going to die. Our medical experts haven't seen any evidence of it. His beard and hair are getting longer and snow white. All this tells us he's, at least, aging more rapidly than usual. How can we understand all this? Let's go back to Doctor Markus, an expert in this area.'

'One can never be an expert in dying,' he answered. 'A Freudian believes that sometimes in our lives we have our death wish, wishing ourselves to be dead. Perhaps, Mr Cougar is merely expressing that wish. And he obviously has an innate desire to die. Nobody can tell whether he'll die today or tomorrow. Dying is a process of life. It's nothing to be scornful about. And yet, it isn't something anybody would like to welcome. We mostly work with family members, helping them cope with death. Earlier in the program, I saw Mr Cougar's daughter, Catherine. She needs all the help she can get. She really suffers psychologically.'

'Do you think he's happy to die?' asked the announcer. 'Would you say he welcomes death, wholeheartedly and without any shackles?'

'From what I heard so far, it seems he's ready for it. In all my professional years, I've never met anybody who is ready for death.'

'You wouldn't say he's ready to die?'

'Isn't it better to ask Mr Cougar? But his dying is causing a national impact on everyone. As I see death, we've the tendency to take it as something mysterious, the other side of life. Nobody ever comes back and tells us what it's like. Because of this, people are interested in Cougar dying. He's tackling the most dreadful fear in us. And that's the cornerstone of life. Anyway, I'm not very occupied by all of this, but I'd like to know how he acquires this insight about himself.'

'In other words, you believe he's stating the truth?'

'It's not so much a question about truth. Oh, no! Our science about death is primitive. We're ignorant about death. If we could see our death coming tomorrow, we'd try to live differently. Wouldn't we?'

The announcer did not like being put in this position, having to express his opinion instead of mediating those of others. 'You're on the line? What's your question?' he asked a caller.

'I'm happy to be on your show. You're doing an excellent job. I don't want to say that Mr Cougar is a charismatic person. What's important in all this is how a little unknown community could grip the entire nation. It makes our society more cohesive and integrated. It brings the generation gap closer. It binds everyone: seniors, middle age, adults, young adults, children—all together. This Cougar reminds me of the *Machiavellian Prince* with his power to grip people and to manipulate them.'

As the speaker searched for words, the commentator intervened, 'Wouldn't you say he makes people believe in him? And at the same time, he doesn't want us to identify ourselves with death? So he's the good prince.'

'Yes. But he could really cause conflict in people. Everybody wants to believe in him; and yet, they doubt whether he can do it. I agree with you. The good prince is doing something inconceivable and incomprehensible. His death suggests a reality to us. And in turn, we learn how to live with ourselves.

'Don't forget the power of the prince. Not so long ago, we practiced colonization through divide and rule. Nowadays, we're doing the same thing: confuse and rule. With all respect to Mr Cougar, he isn't practicing politics, but something real. Real enough to horrify most of us. Oh, yes, if I must say, I'm a bit troubled by all this. Being objective, isn't so easy to me. I just can't separate how meaningful my family is for me. Anyway, we can know whether it'll be darkness or light in due course.'

'Do you have any questions?'

'No, thank you.'

'The new development about Mr Cougar is: he went international a while ago. And people have already started with the countdown. The world is synchronizing its time to our time zone. Let's hear what our listeners have to say and how they've been affected by all this,' cried the announcer. 'Hello, you're on the air.'

'Death, I've experienced a lot of death in my family. My wife died a year ago. My daughter of cancer. My two grandchildren through accidents,' stammered an old man. 'In my eight-six years, I tell you there's been no warning. When it comes, you're gone. This Cougar, chap, he doesn't know anything about death. He doesn't know what's he talking about…'

'Excuse me, sir. Would you like to ask one of our guests a question?' asked the announcer. The speaker could not hear the question because a technician had cut him off. 'Ok, our caller hung up. You're on the air.' He took the next call.

'I'm proud to call myself a Christian,' cried the speaker. 'The priest couldn't be any more right. Nobody knows when he'll die—only God does. Maybe God is telling us something through him. Mr Cougar is one of the bravest men, a real model for all of us. I feel like if he doesn't die, I'd like to be in his place.' He hung up quickly because of his tears.

'Thank you for sharing your feelings with us.'

'That speaker hits something on the nail,' interrupted Dr Markus. 'If I may use the expression. Nobody wants to see Mr Cougar a liar. We do feel deeply sorry for him. And at the same, we don't want him to leave us. All this internal conflict we have is because we want to know him a bit better. We want to be friends of his before he goes. He could teach us something. His death would be a lost for us. And yet, we don't want him to betray us. Now, I'm asking myself about my values in life. How I'd like to be treated. And how important it *is* to have genuine friends.'

'We'll go to our next caller.'

A young man in his late twenties was on the line. 'I'm sorry for Mr Cougar, but I'm not sentimental at all. I think this is a rotten conspiracy. The RCMP and the CIA are pulling a fast one on us. We have a lot of old people these days. They're eating out of the government's pockets. The government had brainwashed poor Mr Cougar to be a hero. Oh, yes, a fearless hero of death. This is awful and disgusting. Telling old people to let go of their lives. All this crap because it's too expensive for the government. And what's more, that's why his identity remains incognito. In the most inhumane actions, you'll find the government has its hands in. And this isn't any exception!'

'Would anyone like to comment on his view?' the announcer asked his guests.

'This is a bit too farfetched,' answered the lawyer. 'The patient is definitely conscious. And he's aware of his surroundings. From all available accounts, we can tell he's responsible for all of his actions. Mr Cougar's family would deny such accusations. His entire community is behind him. The RCMP and CIA involvement is absurd. Our information shows that the police haven't got any records about Mr Cougar's life. And they believe that he's a foreign spy.'

'You're on the air,' called the mediator.

'If anybody deserves any respect, it's Mr Cougar. He's honest. His message is pure. He doesn't look for any gain. No credit, and no psychological praise. He can't take anything with him to the grave. He wants absolutely nothing. All our lives people do things for some gain. Don't we seek materialistic values for everything we do? Let's look at the fact: he knows he'll die, and he wants to say farewell to his loved ones and close friends. He wants to tell all of his friends, thank them for their contribution to his life. He has brought out the true human in us.

'It's amazing! He doesn't look for financial compensation through dying. If we can't trust his words anymore, that tells us we've a lot to learn about ourselves. Mr Cougar wants to say goodbye while he has a chance to do it. People like him are truly genuine. He's making lifetime friends in all sort of weather. Today, we need a microscope to look for solid and precious human beings. Mr Cougar is a rare breed. Can't we see that he doesn't need any material compensation for his actions? Without any reservations, I believe him, and he reminds me that each person has his own rare qualities. He has watered the little dries-up rose bush in me. Those who know how to live also know how to live forever. Mr Cougar is an inspiration for me. He taught me to know myself, my wants, my limits, and how it's important to have friends.'

'Thank you for your comments. Do you have any questions for our guest speakers?' asked the announcer.

'Mister Blackman, you've missed my point,' the caller continued. 'He's given us all the answers to life. One death is sufficient in life. How many more should we expect? How should it be dished out? Look at us. Before we die, we perish in significance. We die before we're actually dead. I don't think you've listened to Mr Cougar, have you?'

Though she was cut off for the next speaker, the announcer summed everything up. 'We recognize the fact that Mr Cougar is quite hospitable, not even sour and bitter toward anyone. We need your opinion of this incredible event.' And the next caller came on:

'How is it possible that there isn't any record of Mr Cougar's life? On the radio, they said he isn't a native Canadian,' cried a hasty speaker. 'Where does he come from? Who are his parents? The police know everything about unimportant people. Are we paying them to sleep on the job? Even the immigration department has a deaf ear. Does he pay taxes like everybody else? It's queer that nobody around here knows him. For sure, we've more questions than answers. I don't swallow all this baloney that he's an alien. He's flesh and blood like all of us,' she finished. And hastily hung up.

The psychiatrist felt forced into a position to shed some light on the matter. 'Today we hardly believe anyone. We're accustomed to having hard facts about a person. His life must be like a portfolio. Where he was born? Which group does he affiliate himself with? What are his earnings? Having all this information about one person, then we might associate ourselves with another person. A great majority of us don't want to know whether a person likes flowers, jazz or the blues. All these add more mysteries to a person. We want to trash away mystery, to bring the hidden into the open, so we can look at it piece by piece.'

'Thank you, for enlightening us more. We've another speaker,' interrupted the announcer.

'My God! Can't anybody be poetic and romantic anymore? Mr Cougar is real, and a Canadian too. We Canadians just mellow in, like a calm ocean at every shore, with a soft and refreshing breeze blowing on us. We've an adorable personality and character in the world. Can it be true that Canadians live in Sandreef? Look at us! We aren't pushy, reckless, and hasty like our southern neighbor. We're very careful; in clear water our thoughts sparkle. We dazzle and roam endlessly in all seasons. Oh yes, Mr Cougar reminds me of how to forge a true Canadian identity without stirring the water. How often are we asked what's it's like to be a Canadian? A nation living like a community. It takes a dying man to awaken the community in all of us. You see how everybody is knitted together. A single thought running through all of us. And it can't be swallowed up easily by the storm. Canadianism is a way of life: being hospitable in the worst winter storm. Its diversity is like shades of snow; it glitters uniquely in the world.

'Cougar dying tells us about a Canadian's feet growing golden roots. That's Cougar, for us! Not a mystic, a billionaire, nor a Hollywood celebrity, but a simple person living a simple life. And he's satisfied with his ways until his dying bed.'

'Thank you, sir, for your lengthy speech. It's quite moving, I must say touching too.'

'Talking about the heritage questions,' interrupted Ms Merville, 'the less rash, hospitable, and diverse cultures. Trapped between big brother and the Arctic Ocean: the native questions couldn't run away, nor the French speaking culture. All this isn't so cut and dry. One thing for sure, we've a complex-people nation. If I understood the speaker correctly, a community unifies all. I don't get it. Why does he stop here? Community exists in everyone. It crosses all borders. So, this community exists within. And Mr Cougar lives within us. Holding all the neighborhoods together. So we're like fishes in the ocean. We can't see the water, but the medium runs through all the fishes equally.'

'You're on the air, who am I speaking to?' asked the announcer.

'I'm calling from Vancouver. Your discussion is quite interesting. We'd like to have more information of what's actually happening with Cougar. The little box on the screen should be bigger. I'm fascinated by how he ages. I can see it, feel it all over me. My back is aching. I can't stand straight without pain, or scratch my back. My skin is peeling. My teeth are shaking. My eyes are foggy. My ears can't break down sound anymore. Why does he age so quickly?' cried a young speaker.

'Thank you! Our technicians will attend to this matter of a bigger score. As you can see, Mr Cougar is still lying in bed. His vital signs are regular. Let's go to our next speaker, you're on the air.'

'I'll feel very worried and hurt if he dies. Whenever he goes into those trances, I feel like I'm going down with him. I want to shake him up. Wake him up. I want to warn him about those trances. He should stay away from them. I feel so helpless, and I can't tell him. If it weren't for those monitors telling me he's still alive, I don't know what would happen to me. I might have a nervous breakdown. As I'm talking to you, right now, I'm shivering and shaking with fear. When he woke up from those spells, I felt much better. It'll be awfully terrible, if we lose him like this. My fear is, will he really die?' she asked as she saw the patient's eyes closing again. She knew another trance was coming, and Mr Cougar was going right into it. The phone drifted away from her mouth, and the monitors did not detect any changes.

The announcer was silent for several seconds as he carefully watched the patient disappear into an unknown zone. He quickly realized himself and tired to hide his subjective feelings for Mr Cougar. 'Yes, we're back on the air. We've just lost our speaker. She left us an intriguing question. Would anyone like to comment on her question?' he asked his guest speakers. The patient's periodic spell had carried them away, too.

'Either way, we'll be losers,' the astronomer sadly whispered, 'If he dies, we'll perish a remarkable person. And if he doesn't die, we'll be left empty handed. It'll shatter our hopes. And our disappointment will be unbearable. My God, what am I saying? It's sickening to wish Mr Cougar a happy and everlasting death.' He showed his confusion and conflicting thoughts. The TV program went on until five o'clock; believers and non-believers were interested in the outcome, and the curiosity of his trance had heightened their sensibility. It was a dark world in which demons prowl and dismembered sinners' bodies awaited the patient. So horrible it was, that a fugitive unconsciously buried it a hundred lifetimes behind him. Luckily, the duration of Mr Cougar's trance lasted for only a minute, and he got out of it pleasantly.

'Ralph, you made a promise to everyone. Do you know anything about the afterlife?' the Timeman asked, waiting for Mr Cougar to answer him.

'What's there is to know?' Edwin challenged. 'Look what you're doing to us. Isn't this a good example of afterlife? I would be able to see others' thoughts and feelings without being able to influence them. I really don't know whether all this is real. You can just cause them in us. We're having experiences of seeing others without their being able to see us. We're like gods, the helpless ones.'

'Have you already forgotten your grandpa's promise?'

'You're very tricky. Yes, my grandpa said that he would die today. Now, you want us to make another promise that he would keep his first promise. There is no need to make a second promise.'

'You aren't answering me, young man!'

'What do you want to hear? Everybody already knows it. Why

can't you accept it, too? My grandpa is an honest man. He respects everyone like himself. Yes, he made a promise to himself and others. At that time, he wholeheartedly believed that he could fulfill his promise of dying. Isn't all this clear enough for you?'

'And what does he believe now?'

'Timeman, my grandpa has seen that human social morality is deteriorating at a rapid pace. And he wants to show us the meaning for living. Each individual has a soul. And the afterlife is about our community remembering us. So, we must strive for intrinsic values.'

'But not everybody welcomes your grandpa's dying!'

'That's natural,' answered Mr Cougar. 'Whenever something different comes along, some people are followers, some are disbelievers, some are indifferent, and others are standbys. It's healthy to have critics.'

'That's true,' interrupted Edwin. 'Life isn't a debate around an ivory table, nor a dangerous beast that has to be kept in a cage. And it's not a fragile glass that must be protected by material values. Life is nothing less than adopting the principle of the soul. But for you, it's a person's last wish.'

'You're talking about life. Have you ever seen any darkness in your own heart?' asked the Timeman.

'I don't have anything to hide. I'm proud of myself. And my grandpa is proud of himself, too.'

'Let's start off with you, young man.'

'OK, show what I already know about myself,' replied Edwin. Mr Cougar made a sign to Edwin, telling him not to dare the Timeman. They made observations around the living room.

15:00 *Janet and Marion*

Janet Cole, who was Edwin's friend, was seventeen years old and going to St Michel High School in town. She was utterly burnt out from fatigue before swimming furiously against the tide outside, and the crowd was of no help in her delicate situation. Perspiring in her black jacket and too exhausted to take any interest in her surroundings, she finally felt relief in Mr Cougar's apartment. She walked around aimlessly like an abandoned child. Expecting to see Mr Cougar in his bedroom with his family, she rechecked herself, was surprised when she noticed someone like a Santa Claus lying in Mr Cougar's living room. He smiled, but his beard concealed it from her. She thought that she was hallucinating about her immoral actions several hours ago. Not recognizing Mr Cougar, the image of that frozen Santa added an extra burden on her fiery temperament that was already overloaded with anger, hate, stress, discomfort, and fatigue. She wanted to find Edwin as fast as possible and then hide herself from everyone. She did not see him, but she could not help taking another quick glance at the snowman in Mr Cougar's bed.

All this time Janet did not escape Catherine, who was staring at her as though Janet had committed a hideous crime. Janet's bursting in did not remove Catherine's burden and suffering; worsened Catherine's nightmare. Catherine wondered what else could happen to her now, for embarrassments were piling up on her. She was not prepared for Janet's intrusion, and her presence also overcast a layer of dark cloud on Marion's heart.

Janet finally recognized Catherine who avoided eye contact with her. Janet was still looking mindlessly into the room until she saw

Marion coming over: 'Hi Marion. I've never seen so many people around here. If I hadn't told the crowd outside that I was pregnant, and that I was part of the family, I'd never have gotten in here. And who is that religious freak lying there?' They both turned and faced Mr Cougar. He was observing them attentively. Marion glanced bluntly at Janet who was continuously passing her right hand on her stomach. As Janet nearly touched her pelvis area, she had forgotten that there was anyone else in the room; she felt like she was being tortured and was awfully disgusted about what she did. Naturally, Catherine gave her a dirty look, and she thought that Janet had secretly planned to trap her son, and Edwin fell into it.

'Yes, Janet! It isn't funny, at all! Why don't you disappear to where you come from? And you know darn well that's Grandpa,' cried Marion angrily. Catherine felt that Janet had no right to disrupt their personal pain and suffering.

Janet stared at her in surprise and felt like a merciless butcher of everything innocent and harmless. 'What else do you have to torment us with? You've already broken up our family. Now, you're insulting my mother. How dare you?' Marion did not mind that others were listening to her, for Janet's face sang out in bewilderment.

But Marion saw it differently and then cried out: 'You're a nameless intruder. You embarrass my family, and now you're humiliating my grandpa's dying bed.'

'Listen, Marion,' Janet halfheartedly defended, 'I don't know why everybody is so jumpy at me. You want to take my throat, then take it. It's yours. I haven't done anything to you.' Janet took a repugnant glance at Mr Cougar, and his brilliant inviting eyes gave her a warm welcome and hello. 'So, it's Mr Cougar. How do you expect me to know that?' she questioned.

'Hello, Mr Cougar, bon voyage!' she unenthusiastically greeted him without showing any intention of speaking to him, and her curiosity about his physical appearance did not sink in right away.

'You've said your hello, now leave. We don't want your kind around here, Janet.'

Janet hesitated awhile, as she recollected hearing something about

Mr Cougar's condition on the radio. For seeing him was unbelievable. From the way he looked, she thought that he would not be able to recognize her. She, nonetheless, gave him a smile, and he nodded his head sluggishly in acknowledgement. She was taken by surprise that he recognized her. She took another quick glance at him, and then she entertained doubts that the person she saw before her was really Mr Cougar.

Marion's defensive position tightened up to protect her family, as she believed that she was opposing a slimy arrogant creature that should crawl back in its filthy hole. 'So, Miss Cole, what kind of horror do you want to push down our throat today? Don't tell me you've found an apartment in town? What is it, Janet? Are you waiting for the ring?'

'Come on, Marion! Why are you so edgy? I've known you all my life. What's getting into you?'

'How can you be so barefaced?' she whispered the question for only Janet.

'My God, Marion! I've known you all my life. I'm the same Janet. I haven't changed,' she begged, appealing to their old friendship. They'd been extremely close together since their childhood,, sharing the same secret of life with plans to encounter the same future. But their friendship gradually disappeared when Edwin entered into the picture. He started going out with Janet, and Marion felt that Janet had used her to get her brother.

'Listen, Janet, I know your type. Don't try to soften me up. It won't work. If I hadn't known you before—your kind! Just go, will you? Why don't you go and leave us alone?'

Janet's natural response was to tell Marion off. But she felt obligated to put everything in perspective since most people in the room periodically attended to their conversation and thought that Janet would leave. And Mr Cougar was watching them. That softened Janet.

But Mr Cougar influenced the mourners differently in the room. Some believed that he wheeled mystical power, and they were afraid of it, the unknown. And they did not want to disturb him in his dying bed. Some honestly believed he could not do it, for death could not be mastered by any human beings. Others truly showed their respect and friendship for a person who they had known and shared their life with. Marion noticed that her grandpa was impressed by their argument, so she called Janet aside to an empty room in which Edwin sometimes slept. Janet felt relief, and she did not mind leaving the patient with his fatalistic course.

They left the door slightly open, 'I couldn't find your brother anywhere. I really have to speak to him, it's urgent,' murmured Janet. She felt guilty that Edwin had to carry her burden. Because of her, Edwin's family was quarrelling, and he had to confront all sorts of sour faces at home and in the streets. She nodded her head in disbelief and wiped her tears before Marion could see right through her. She felt a strong urge to tell Marion the truth. But she was not sure whether Marion was still her best friend. Feeling all alone and depressed, her heart was about to burst open like autumn leaves tumbling in the wind, but Marion interrupted her:

'Janet, we can't be friends anymore. Because of what you've done, nobody wants to be near you. How low can you get? How could you do such a thing to my brother? If you've forgotten our secret, then I haven't. You always told me you could coerce anybody against his will. Just get pregnant! And he's your, forever! This isn't much of a secret anymore. So, you did it! For your information, nobody can forget this kind of stuff,' she said staring at Janet who recalled every single word in embarrassment.

Janet remained speechless, as she entertained the thought that their friendship ended here. She was too weak to defend herself against Marion's abuses. And her heart was too heavy with the thought that Marion hated her. She wanted to say something, but she could not speak. She desperately needed somebody to lean on at this moment. She remembered how close they were: sharing the same nonsense and talking about emotions and dreams that were taboo for anybody else. Her inner self-protection finally gave way in a feeble voice: 'No, Marion! It isn't Edwin. He isn't the father.'

'What's that? How could you do that to him? My God, you're out of your mind. My poor brother! Now, you want me to keep it a secret. No deal!' She bared her teeth in anger as she spoke. Marion now wanted to restore her family from further public embarrassment and condemnation. As she was preparing to leave, Janet burst into tears.

'No, Marion! Please listen to all of it. Only one second—please!' she pleaded, and she never felt so small and degraded in her life. Marion held a rigid posture, and then she took a few small steps in front of Janet. She felt like punching her in the nose. Since violence was not in her nature, she rechecked herself. Most importantly, she did not want to make a scene.

'It won't work! It's over, get it?'

'Marion, Edwin knows it, too.'

'What? He does? I don't believe you!'

'Yes, I told him.'

'Listen, Janet. Why don't you just say it! And don't give me that innocent crying look.'

'Your brother wanted to help me. To save my image, and my family's too. All this time Edwin had to live with it.'

'You mean to say he knew this all along. That slimy nerd! How could he be so insensitive? He's made Mom suffer so much—all of us. Mom could have died of a heart attack. And it would have been all his fault.'

'I'm sorry. It's all my fault, not his. He said that if things got worse, he'd marry me. And be the father of my child.'

'So, he did, eh!'

'Please, don't be so difficult.'

'So, who is the father?'

'That's the problem.' Janet started to weep again. As her inner strength appeared to have melted away, she crumbled onto Marion for support, embracing her.

'It's Ok, Janet. Everything gonna be Ok. Trust me.' Marion said, as Janet's tears ran down onto her shoulder. Janet regained herself a little and then slowly walked to the little study desk in the room and sat on the chair. Marion felt very sorry for her.

'You remember Rich's birthday party, the boy with a lot of freckles on his face?' Janet asked.

'Yes, but I didn't go to the party because it was in town. And I didn't have anybody to drive me back home.'

'Edwin and I went. But he left early, at ten o'clock or so. He had to keep his grandpa company, like always…. Whenever things are sticky upstairs, he stays here.'

'You mean to say, he isn't the outsider we thought he was. Well, this is news,' she joyfully commented. 'So, what happened at the party?'

'Well, after he left, I met a new boy, Bruno. We were dancing and having so much fun together. After I had some beer, and gin and tonic, I wasn't doing so great. And besides that, it was getting late. So he drove me home. And we made out in his car,' she started to weep. She wiped her puffy face on her jacket sleeves. 'For once, in my whole life, I've lost myself! How terrible I felt afterward! I started to blame your brother for leaving me alone at the party. Anyway, I didn't tell him what had happened. My secret wasn't much of a secret for long. Six weeks later I told him that I might be pregnant. Who else could I tell? I don't have anybody else to talk to. I trust Edwin. He could hold a secret. We're only friends, That's all, Marion. He wasn't angry with me. He only asked me how he could help without demoralizing me.

'The girls at school noticed that I was vomiting once or twice a day. I was so edgy with all of them. Even smoking made me vomit. In the canteen I was so picky about what I ate. I was so sensitive to the smell of food. All this time, I didn't tell anybody else, but the girls at school teased me of possibly being pregnant. When I was buying the self-test for pregnancy at the pharmacy in town, I guess someone saw me. After that, the whole community was whispering their discovery. They put one and one together, and the answer was Edwin—the father. With your brother, the world could tumble under his feet, and he wouldn't show any fear. Nothing is too heavy for him. He doesn't even regret what he does for me. He didn't try to convince others that he wasn't the father. With him, either he's thinking or doing nothing. He hardly shows any depression or regret in his life. Why am I saying this? He's your brother, and you know him.'

'So, where's Bruno?' Marion asked politely.

'When I knew that I was pregnant, everyday I went to town. Without eating anything, I patrolled each street, restaurant, and bar in town. I was all alone out there, crying at every street corner. Honestly, I didn't know what I was doing anymore. I couldn't remember where I slept overnight. Luckily, your brother found me wandering. Yes, Marion, Edwin brought me home. It was awful. In my rags I was in every street, hotel, motel, and bar. I don't know how I did it without any food or a cent in my pocket. If it hadn't been for Edwin, I don't know what would have happened to me. For sure, I'd have gone down the drain. I went everywhere, but I never saw Bruno again. Rick told me he doesn't know any Bruno. He might have been a visitor who crashed parties and went away.

'My family took the news as expected. I was the most deadly disease on earth. They don't speak to me. When I sat in the living room, everybody disappeared. I ate when nobody was around. They wished I were dead for what I'd caused them to endure and suffer in this little hole. You already know this. Nobody, not even you, Marion, said hello to me in the street. To lessen my pain sometimes, Edwin brought me here to eat and sleep on the couch in the living room. That's why he was looking at us like that. He knows everything.'

'Who?'

'Your grandpa. He's a very kind man. He didn't mind when I slept here. In the morning, I had to leave early, so none of you would find out. That's why your brother usually brings down your grandpa's breakfast.'

'My grandfather knows about it, too?'

'Yes! He said, "Life is virtuous, and nobody can destroy it. This could make any heart humble." He told me that he didn't know our generation anymore. And he's dying too quickly, now.'

'What are going to do with the baby?'

'Your grandpa gave me the address of a souvenir store in St John. At the store, I should ask for White-Cloud Spirit. I went there this morning after Edwin grabbed something for me to eat. At the store, an old native Indian gave me another address to go to. From there some people from an Indian reservation took me to another place. That Indian woman looked very old. Maybe, she was much older than she really looked. Anyway, she told me that she knew your grandpa very well, and that he was waiting for me. So, I've just came back from her place.'

'What did you do there, Janet?'

'Nothing special.' Janet started to cry again. 'She told me to lie down on her mat without any clothes on. She mumbled something several times. And then she rubbed my stomach very lightly. It took only five minutes. Five minutes…' she repeated and stopped speaking as tears started to pour down. The more she tried to wipe them off, the faster they came down all over her cheek.

'Janet, I don't know what you're getting at.'

'After that, I felt like going to the toilet. I trembled, when a glowing light passed though me. I saw myself as a little girl running and lying around in the field. A warm breeze blew my hair. Warm grass tickled the bottom of my feet. Those were the days when I used to lie in the field and look up in the sky. I tried to count all the butterflies flying by. To see how they flew, I used to chase after them in the high grass. There was this innocent one in the thick green grass, more beautiful than all the other ones. I couldn't get close to it. I thought it was teasing me, and then it told me I wasn't ready for it yet!'

'My dear, Janet! I feel so sorry. You had to do all this alone. You're very courageous,' said Marion, holding back her feelings toward Janet.

'At midday, she told me to hurry back before it was too late. On my way back, I hated your grandpa so much. And at the same time, I know I should be thanking him. On the radio, I heard something like he wanted to die. I couldn't concentrate on anything. I couldn't remember my name, but I slowly came around it. When I saw all those people outside, I couldn't be angry with him. I don't really care to see him either. I didn't come here to thank him. I wanted to see Edwin. Curiously, when I looked at your grandpa in his eyes, I think he knew what I've done.'

'I don't know what to say, Janet. You had a shock. By chance do you happen to know the woman's name?'

'No, Marion! I don't know if she said her name. I can't remember.'

'It's Ok. I was just thinking how helpful she could be to so many women in your situation.'

'Now, everything is finished. I've given myself a scar which I can't forget.'

'Are you going to tell your parents you've had an abortion?'

'In this small place, when you tell one person your secret, the whole community knows it too. For sure, I know one thing. I love Edwin. I owe my life to him. But his freedom is more important. Now he's free from all bondage. There's nothing to tie him down to one place. I guess he never says how he feels about me.'

'Sorry, Janet! I can't help you here. This is between you and him. Keep me out of it, please.'

'I guess if he loved me, he'd never tell me. Well, there's something strange about him. I think he has a mysterious aroma around him. He doesn't talk much. When he found me in town, he said "Janet, I'm here to take you home." I cried, shouted, and swore at him. I called him all sorts of names, but he didn't move. He looked at me with his stone dry face. Then he said: "Well if you aren't coming tonight, then tomorrow. If not tomorrow, then next week or in two months. When you've decided, we'd go home together." I should say that true Cougar's blood runs in his veins. He always says the right thing at the right moment to me. I don't know how he does it.'

'So, he knows, you've had an abortion, I guess.'

'No, he doesn't! That's why I'm here. I want to talk to him. Where is he?'

'Ask Lewis, if you can,' Marion reaffirmed. She knew that he was still busy with a reporter.

'Listen, Marion, I have to see if I can have a word with him,' Janet said very courageously, and she went to the doorway where Lewis was being interviewed with a telescope that was held backward.

Edwin was speechless after what he had seen. He realized that he didn't know what he could have done to help Janet. His silence did not last long: 'She loves you,' cried the Timeman.

Edwin murmured, "Yes, she loves me," and continued to look hypnotic.

'Edwin, get hold of yourself,' cried Mr Cougar.

'Yes, as I was saying,' cried Edwin, trying to overcome his sentiment. 'She loves me for what I have done. And for what she has seen in me. It's natural that she loves me in her moment of distress. Remember, she doesn't love me for love's sake, or see me as a lover. Because of her kindness, she wants to make the sacrifice to live with me. But that doesn't come from true love.'

'That isn't the way you used to behave whenever you were with her,' interrupted the Timeman.

'Oh, don't tell me you're also a spy!'

'You don't want to confess the truth because we are here. And the truth is—you think and feel one way, but you behave differently. Isn't this natural in human beings?'

'Are we still taking about love?'

'No. Most people think that community soul is a good thing. But they aren't motivated to act according to the principle of the soul. They participate in social morality because of some external forces. Consequences and penalties steer human beings, not virtue. And if someone's act is driven internally, the depth is very shallow. Because there is some sort of psychological reward to obtain. People don't act morally just because it is the right thing to do in society. And if anyone does, he'll be swallowed up by counter forces in society, like businesses and governments.'

'Are you telling me that businesses and governments don't operate with a common sense view of morality?' asked Mr Cougar. 'I think they accept certain fundamental human values. Though businesses and governments influence our lives, community soul is not strictly confined to those forces. It is about having friends, too. And wanting to be remembered positively. We act freely. It would be very dangerous if we didn't question our social morality. Questioning our community values could advance us and allow us to grow.'

'Ralph, you're trying to defend your grandson. How interesting. You are not listening very well, are you? People don't live in harmony. They repay their debts because they want more loans.'

'If social morality has stumbled from its pedal tool, it's about time my grandpa tried to re-promote it. Whenever friendship loses its significance, other values creep in to fill in the gap. And my grandpa has tried to do something about the deterioration of our essential values.'

'Wouldn't you say that your grandpa has his first victim? He contributes to murder. Is this how the principle of the soul works?' Edwin was about to rebut the Timeman when Mr Cougar intervened.

'We believe in doing an act which carries the least negative consequence. I try to show Janet other courses of action. Though she made the final decision to have an abortion, what I did was human. I value each life as being precious. She wanted to commit suicide, killing herself and the baby, or to have an abortion. She had already consulted a doctor in town and made the final arrangement. When she asked me if I knew someone else who performed abortions, I couldn't lie to her. I had to tell her the truth.

'Philosophers might condemn my action by using ethical theories or religions. I should have ignored her pledge. I couldn't ignore my conscience. Because I experience guilt, I had to say something to her. Very painfully, Janet decided on her life. She would feel the loss of her self-identity in whatever action she chose. Her community would have chastised her if she had had the baby or had had an abortion. Janet is much more courageous than I am in facing life and death.'

'Ralph, does a fetus have a community soul, too?'

'Janet's action couldn't run away from her. It would live with her for a very long time. It would be a constant reminder of how her life would have been. For sure, Janet would keep that soul alive as long as she lives. Had our community shown some more compassion and understanding toward her, she might have acted differently. Her actions are a critical evaluation of the current values of society. And tolerance must be incorporated in our community soul.'

'Grandpa, I am to be blamed for her mess. I left her at the party. And I should have married her,' cried Edwin, pitying himself. The Timeman was deliberately trying to undermine both Edwin's and Mr Cougar's self-integrity in order to ridicule their principle of community soul.

'Ralph, let me dethrone you some more. Your life isn't innocent. You have also crucified your best friend to a meaningless existence. Sit back and listen carefully,' said the Timeman.

15:15 William's Conflicting Friendship

Someone had mistakenly stumbled over the electric cord and disconnected the camera. Within a few seconds it had been re-plugged and it sent out a burst of electric current that affected the cameras' focus on the mourners. William's life was adjusted from a background view on the horizon to the image of a local hero. He had changed into a celebrity, for he held the secret of Mr Cougar's life. People would pay most to anything to have his story. Janet came closer to the outside living room door and waited; she had no intention of disturbing the live interview.

'Don't call me Mr William. Lewis will do,' cried Lewis. His partly gray beard, only a week old, and his long oily hair had not been washed for a few days. Looking older than his age, he could not hide his carefree bachelor life.

'Mr William. Excuse me, Lewis. You're Mr Cougar's best friend, aren't you? So you're very close to him, wouldn't you say?' asked Miss Cook.

He looked at the patient and then to Miss Cook: 'If you want to say so, then that's it.' He was indirectly telling her that he was a very proud person and unwilling to reveal any information about his friend.

'Lewis,' she blushed, 'our listeners are dying to know Mr Cougar some more. You can really assist us, sir.'

'Well then if you put it that way, I can only say what I've seen with my own eyes. I won't give you any cock-and-bull story about my pal,' he said, showing some reservation about his young friend wanting to die.

'When did you first meet him? And how?'

'Yes, I'm getting there, can't you see lady! You people are so pushy and nosy. You want to know a person's life in less than a minute. You want me to tell you about his youthful days when he could move a mountain with only a bucket in two words? It ain't so easy. I was a hired hand when everything started. I was working for Catherine's grandfather, Mr Winfred.' He seemed to drift away into his past, reliving a few precious moments about Mr Winfred's daughter. 'That's Marina's maiden name. Oh, she was really something. The most beautiful gal I've even seen. We used to call her deep blue. Oh, those eyes were full of animal magnetism. Her long sandy blonde hair nobody could ever forget. It sang in the wind.'

'Excuse me, sir. We're talking about Mr Cougar, if you don't mind. We know Mrs Cougar was a ravishing woman. Unfortunately, she died recently.'

'Yes, Ralph was a very lucky man. She was like a sister to me. I always had to look out for her. I was much older than her. And if you didn't know it yet, she was an only child.'

'Thank you, Mr William. Mr Cougar must have been a handsome young man to sweep her off her feet.'

He stared at the reporter as though he was collecting some more scattering images and assembling them like a tailor working with unequal pieces. 'Well, it all started one afternoon. We were coming home later than usual with the incoming tide. From where we were, we could see the harbor. As we came in slowly, we thought at first a capsized boat was coming in with the tide. It was about one nautical mile behind us. Then it passed us at the same distance. We tried to follow it as fast as possible. But it was moving toward shore faster. It somehow kept the same distance beside us. Some of the other boats said that they had seen that huge patch in the water moving around them as though it wanted to lead them to shore. Whenever they tried to get near it, it moved away. As we got closer to shore, the boat sank. Then Jimmy, Marina's father, said he saw something on the shore. He insisted that there was a survivor lying on the shore. My God, when we got nearer, it looked like a person lying stone dead on the shore. We quickly forgot how he'd gotten there. Jimmy asked me to take the boat very close to the shore, he jumped into the water and got to him first. I, and the other fishing boats went to the dock. Then we hurried back to help out.

Ralph was lying there. For sure, everybody thought he was as dead as a rock, but not Jimmy! He tried to pump his stomach out while we just stood around. We thought he was dead. But Jimmy wouldn't stop, so we just looked at him. Jimmy was as stubborn as a mule. He was convinced that Ralph was still alive. But his skin was white like chalk. When Jimmy rubbed his skin too hard, it peeled off like paper. So, he had to be careful. Finally, Jimmy took his cell phone and phoned the hospital for an ambulance. Everybody thought he was crazy. From looking at Ralph's body in front of us, Jimmy should have phoned the morgue instead.'

'How did Mr Winfred know he wasn't dead?'

'It looked as though Ralph had been in the water for several days. The salt water had peeled off some of his skin. Because he wasn't swollen up at all, Jimmy believed that he was still alive. Mind you, reporter lady, Ralph didn't have any pulse or heart beat. When the ambulance people came, they laughed at us for calling them. They took their time loading him in. They knew there wasn't any hurry to bury the dead. This made Jimmy very angry. Jimmy and I went with him in the back of the ambulance. The two medics were in the front, maybe laughing at us.

As the ambulance crawled back to town, it happened right in front of our own eyes. You wouldn't believe it even if I'm gonna say it to you right now. Yes, it was so scary for us. His skin changed to a normal color. First it started with his face. When I saw that, I banged for the medics to come and see. They stopped. Oh, they really freaked out. All four of us squeezed ourselves in the back of the ambulance. It was really hot in there. Then one of the medics removed Ralph's blanket. We could see how his body was slowing changing color in his neck, arms, belly, and feet. The ambulance people didn't know what to do. So, they rushed us to the hospital. The emergency doctor told us that what we saw was normal because Ralph's blood was circulating normally again.'

'How long did he stay in hospital?'

'Three or four days at the most. He was unconscious. The doctor said he was in a coma just like the ones he's having now. But Ralph woke up from his coma in less that one day. He was in a terrible shock. The doctor told us that Ralph had a little brain damage. With all the water that he took in, we were lucky he was alive. Because Ralph suffered from a slight brain damage, he couldn't remember his past. And everything was left at that.

'After the hospital, Jimmy and I promised never to reveal his secret to anyone, especially to people in our community. You wouldn't believe what Jimmy told the doctor. He said that Ralph was working for him, and that he fell overboard. I'm not sure if Jimmy stole Ralph's medical records from the hospital. Because the police couldn't find any record of Ralph. They didn't press the issue either. They knew that Ralph had lost his memory. So they looked for someone to match his description. And then his records were pushed aside and forgotten.'

'How did you know his name?'

'That was easy. He had on a strange chain and pendant around his neck. I think that Jimmy took it off when Ralph was lying on the shore. Some strange language was written on the pendant, so whatever letters Jimmy could make out it came to "Ralph Cougar." Jimmy gave him back his golden chain and pendant when he became conscious.'

'What language did he speak?'

'For a long time he didn't speak at all. But he understood us. He really knew a lot about fishing. For a while he lived at Jimmy's place. Then Ralph rented a room at Jimmy's and worked as a hand on the boat.'

'Did Marina teach him English?'

'Oh, no! He started to speak just like that, perfect English. I guess at first he didn't want to speak. Maybe he didn't want to talk about himself. You know how some people are, don't you? Back then, our community was much smaller, and nobody wanted to know who he was. And how he got stranded here. He was here, and that was enough for us.'

'How do you know he was seventeen years old?'

'He still had his born hair. He could have been fifteen or sixteen. Nobody thought about asking him his age.'

'Could he read and write?'

'I guess so. When he was living alone, he did everything for himself. One thing was for sure, he was very smart. Smart enough to hide himself from all of us.'

'Would you say he was a normal person?'

'Yep! He fit in well with our community. He liked to be by himself. Walking on the beach in the evening. Look at him. He couldn't be anymore normal than anybody else in here.' They glanced over at him. Mr Cougar was still conscious and appeared to have been listening to their conversation.

'I heard he used to drink a lot and take his father-in-law's boat out at night. Can you confirm this for us?'

'I told you. Fishing was in his blood. I think that was how he got lost at sea in the first place. Yes, there was a certain wildness in him. Like any young man at his age, he liked adventures.'

'You mean to say, Mr William, he was like a wild beast when he was young?'

'No. Not in that sense. He was daring. He liked going out at night. He didn't show any fear.'

'Did he ever suffer from any sickness? Has he ever been hospitalized, sir?'

'You're talking about a warrior. He doesn't have anytime to be sick.'

'Sir, why do people call him the shark man?' She was not comfortable with this question, but she had to ask it for the public. Lewis stared at the patient and hesitated.

'Sir, please!'

Lewis rubbed his face several times and cleared his throat: 'Ralph and I mostly worked in the boat. Jimmy trusted him more than anyone else. After he came to work with us, we never pulled in a shark, not even a baby one. When the other boats got one in their nets, he exchanged it for a fish. He put it back into the water.'

'Did you ask him why he put them back in the ocean?'

'Is that what you want to know?' he stared at the reporter. 'Listen lady, he's right here. Why don't you ask him yourself? I guess you don't have a clue about fishing. Sharks chase fish into our nets. When we saw sharks the day before, we put our nets around that area. Oh, yes. Sometimes, we couldn't take in all the fish we caught. We had to throw them back into the water.'

'Sir, did he ever go swimming with sharks?'

'I told you. Didn't I?'

'Yes, he was fearless and daring. He went swimming whenever he wished.'

'Not exactly. Sometimes, he plunged into the water and said to me, "See you at the dock." And about a half hour later, he'd show up. Oh, Ralph could swim like a fish. Swimming can really make you fit. That's why he still doesn't have a gram of fat on him. Salt water is the best anti-infection there is. You should try it. It's really good for your skin and health. It also has a magical potion to hide your age. As you know, I can't swim so good.'

'Did you ever see Mr Cougar swim with sharks, sir?'

'I don't know,' he answered hesitantly. 'When you go swimming in the ocean, does anybody ever say to you: Reporter woman, you're swimming with fishes? Don't you swim with everything in the ocean— sharks, crabs, whales, octopus, lobsters, barracudas, and what not? He went swimming whenever he wanted to.

'For the record, Ralph thinks it's much safer to swim with sharks than with piranhas and barracudas. Sharks warn you whenever they're around. They're the only marine life that telephone with their fin. They don't have much fear. Likewise, people shouldn't either. But we show fear and then panic. This way, we're telling them that their meal is running away. You get my point? Most swimmers send back the wrong information. I don't think that Ralph is the type who'd challenge a shark in its own territory.

'Sharks are like us. They're fearless, and they don't have any modesty in obtaining their food. Like scavengers, they'll eat anything. They never lose their honor and respect for that. People eat everything too, but we deny that part of our nature. To any person a shark is the most unimaginable and hideous of creatures. But you forget one thing. People like to be crested, too. It's not only seductive, but also calming and relaxing. It's the best medicine against stress. For sharks, it's mesmerizing. They love it, too.

'Ralph is the terror of time. He's chasing time away. He wants to pack time to his own convenience.'

'Mr William, one of your fishing colleagues said that Mr Cougar jumped into freezing water to free trapped sharks in his net. Is this true?'

'And?'

'Can you comment please?'

'There isn't anything to comment about. It's natural to free a shark from your net. We need these predators to chase their prey into our nets. We want them to do the work for us. Ralph is absolutely correct. He has a lot of respect for these creatures. They serve us with dignity and honor. And their way of life should be respected, too. It takes the most courageous creatures on earth to warn its prey. They aren't like snakes, lions, and humans who hide and linger around dark corners to stake their prey with a quick snap.'

'Are you saying he never held a shark and swam with it for fun?

'Why are you asking me this? Ask him! Look, he's right here! How am I supposed to know this?'

'Sorry, we're just trying to get some information about Mr Cougar. And we appreciate your help for this.'

'You should ask him all these questions, not me. But you don't want to ask him, because he doesn't have much time left. For your information, Ralph is my only true friend. Can't you see how angry I'm with him? And at the same time, I'm very happy for him. With him, I've learned the meaning of love and death.' This revelation surprised the interviewer, for Lewis had revealed much more than he should have.

'We do understand your feelings. You've hated him all your life. Now, you can have a piece of mind. It's not your fault that Marina chose him. But your love for her must be immeasurable. Because you loved only her, you were unable to love another woman. It's terrible to accept how easily Mr Cougar is walking away from it all as a free man. Though you resent him, you still like him.' She was appealing to him as a tragic lover. Lewis did not show any surprise, nor did he care to show any more of his feelings.

'I'm not angry about the past. I want him to feel guilty for marrying Marina. I wish it were me in his dying bed. Then I'd have a chance to tell him how much he made me suffer. How he cheated my life away. I know that he'd crawl to my bed and beg me for forgiveness. If you know how much I'd like him to suffer my pain and agony,' he murmured. For Mr Cougar had won the entire war without fighting any battles.

'Sir, you'd like to take your revenge, wouldn't you?'

'I'm angry with him. Why can't he suffer like me? You know what he told me earlier today? He said that Marina had made her choice. He couldn't ignore her choice, and if he had, he'd have suffered. From his confession, we have the same sentiment toward Marina, and we respect each other. And I admire Ralph for this.

'We both dearly loved the same woman. It must be an old saga in human relationships. That golden crown all humans have to wear. Yes, I'm a tragic loser. I must confess, I did try very hard to win her love. Even though I'd tried so hard, I guess it wasn't hard enough. I don't think Ralph did anything at all. He told me it was difficult for him to be himself, and it'd be impossible for him to be someone else. None of us could imagine an endless struggle, so Marina had to choose one of us. Ralph loves the sea, too. If Marina had chosen me, he'd have gone to sea. Reporter woman, to tell you the truth, all my life, I have waited for the moment to see his pain and suffering; it kept me alive until now. I don't have any substance in me.' He stared at the reporter thinking, she could understand what he was talking about.

'You couldn't marry the person whom you loved the most, so you haven't married at all. Your love for Marina would always be alive. It doesn't get old or young. Love is eternal. Sir, did you ever confront her with your feelings? To get it out in the open?' She tried to stay objective, but she had shifted to the side of the underdog. She thought of herself as a young beautiful woman with a professional career, and she was realistic, too. Nobody could sweep her off her feet. She hoped to find someone like herself without overworking the idea of love. And if there was any love in the package, it would be a blessing for her.

'Talking about all this,' he said painfully, 'cleans me up. Nothing is left in me. I don't hold any resentment. Marina talked to me. We put everything on the level. It was next to impossible for her to choose. But not to go crazy, she had to make a choice. She didn't expect paradise. She'd hoped for a simple life.'

'She was quite a woman. Nobody wouldn't want to be in her place. You wouldn't say that her marriage had been made in heaven, would you?'

Lewis smiled. 'Anybody who married Marina chose to live in harmony. They tried to have a baby boy. If they had, they'd have called the baby Lewis. That's something, isn't it?'

'Yes. Before we go, do you think Mr Cougar will die?'

'Ralph,' he shouted, and then the patient turned and gazed at them sympathetically, 'are the sharks still swimming today?' The question poured new life into him to combat the Timeman.

'Thank you, Lewis!' Cougar responded. 'The past has disowned me. The future closes its gate on my face. My dearest friend, I'm stretched to the limit at both ends. I feel like a lonely star crying out in the night,' he murmured, showing some conscious control over himself.

'Get it?' Lewis snapped at the reporter. 'You have his answer.' He felt sad, for Ralph's death would be unbearable and could drive him insane.

'Sir, we can't understand all this riddle. We need some straight answers—like yes or no,' she said, forcing herself into Lewis' destiny.

'You can't understand him, can you? It's like the fox and the hound story. We have many ways to die, but only one way to live. We see this all around us today, don't we? My friend said there is a way to go too, and it's unique. Each of us has to seek it out—the way. But life is calling him away from death. He can't jump onto its path. I guess, he's prevented from joining it, too.'

'Ladies and gentlemen, you have it! Mr Cougar is up against the ultimate conqueror of all. Very soon, we'll have the answer . Please stay tuned for the latest,' she finished, giving Lewis the message that their interview was over. Lewis turned and was walking toward his friend when Janet stopped him and exchanged a few words. Then he leaned over Mr Cougar, and his tears fell on Mr Cougar's forehead. Lewis buried his head next to Mr Cougar's. Both of them started to cry. Lewis wiped his eyes on Mr Cougar's beard, and then he took his hand and wiped Mr Cougar's eyes. A dark shadow seemed to pass through everyone's heart, and tears were the only reaction. The emotion was too strong for Mr Cougar; he suddenly drifted away from everyone in the living room and took refuge in his subconsciousness—the trance state.

Edwin was very interested in his grandpa's past, especially about how he had gotten to Sandreef. They had never spoken much about it. Lewis' love for his grandma also fascinated Edwin. Mr Cougar stared at Edwin and knew that he had to be accountable to his grandson because he didn't want Edwin to have any doubts in his mind. Speaking about his love wasn't something he wanted to discuss, but he had no choice and started.

'I've nothing to confess. I don't have to hide myself from others. And yet, I am unable to say anything sensible about myself when there are more blank spots in my life than full ones. It appears as though someone else controls my destiny.'

'Ralph, get to the point, will you?' asked the Timeman.

'I never held back my love for my dearest wife. After I lost her, I realize how meaningful my life had been. I also grasped the depth of Lewis' suffering and agony. I knew that by marrying Marina there would be a barrier between Lewis and me. Both of us loved Marina. I suffered because I denied Lewis' happiness. Come to think about it, I'd prefer to be Lewis. He has always been like a dear brother to me.' He stopped speaking abruptly.

'You've nullified friendship. If you hadn't married Marina, Lewis would have been very happy. Ralph, you didn't only destroy a friendship, but you also denied Lewis' happiness. So where is your community soul that you've been preaching about? A phony, you are!'

'I see your point. If Edwin marries Janet, he'll deny another young man's happiness. And at the same time, Edwin will be denying another young woman's happiness if he marries Janet. This is how you want to tell me that people are very egocentric and against each other. There can't be any true friendship among people. And fraternity is empty of meaning. People are unhappy and mistrustful of each other. It would take more than one religion to resolve such hate and unhappiness. Alternatively, we should abolish all religious beliefs about marriage and the entire institution of marriage. After doing all this, our choices and preferences for the opposite sex as permanent or temporary partners might not remove our unhappiness or unfriendliness. If two adults have freely chosen to live together, their relationship should be respected. And a marriage contract is about the union between two individuals.

'If they are philosophical about their decision to live together and denying someone else's happiness, and if they rapture in their relationship because of the other person's happiness, they will be denying their own relationship and happiness. Today most people are not altruistic; we tend to be in a state of confrontation.

'You're saying that marriage is a special type of relationship that undermines our friendships. And you are not talking about the relationship between parents and children, siblings, and strangers as being friendly.'

'Don't try to second-guess me! We don't need community soul. The problem is about denying another's happiness. There can never be true friendship as long as there is marriage. It causes unhappiness when pleasure is denied to others. This is the root of social immorality, unfriendliness, and mistrust among people. Ralph, you can't deny this,' remarked the Timeman.

'Human nature is about affirming one sort of relationship and denying others,' cried Mr Cougar. 'And this is the best we can do because we are bestowed with freedom and choice. As I see it, love between partners is a blessing, the highest human value. But we shouldn't forget Lewis. If we modernize our social morality by abolishing the institution of marriage, people might be friendlier. And community soul might flourish. And yet, doing this is like turning back the clock a few thousand years. On the other hand, we aren't ready for this yet. And there will always be someone like Lewis in any social setting.'

'I really don't see the problem here,' interjected Edwin. 'Community soul is relevant today. Nobody denies Lewis's happiness. He caused his own unhappiness. And if he truly loved my grandma, he should have accepted her happiness as being important. But he was too selfish. He wanted to possess her. And everybody knows that love grows when both people feel the same way about each other. Lewis sees his fault. And he is just crying out his weakness like a little baby.'

'Timeman, friendship is about forgetting old wounds, not reliving them. Lewis overcame his wounds when he spoke to the reporter. One more thing, you're referring to my grandpa's generation, not mine. We are more open. And yet, we need community soul because our friendships are overlooked by materialistic values. Look and see how we live today—stress, overindulgence, and cutting corners. We've too much material things, but less friendship and living with the principle of the soul is a mega society.'

'Although you have stripped me naked,' said Mr Cougar, talking to the Timeman, 'something is still missing. My past is incomplete. And I am ready to confront it.'

'Very modest. How can I show you your past when you can't experience fear, anxiety, loss, death, and human tragedy?'

'Fuse my lower level consciousness with my higher one,' cried Mr Cougar.

'Grandpa, don't do it!' cried Edwin. 'If he could have done it, he would have snatched your entire consciousness away from your body. Don't allow him to possess your mind. I don't trust him.'

'Don't worry, Edwin. My mind won't wander very far. As soon as it is threatened, it'll rush back for security.'

'I have to face my adversary, regardless of the consequences. Pray for me, Edwin.'

'Good, I'll reunite you with your body,' answered the Timeman, 'and then I'll separate your consciousness from your surroundings. You'll be able to see your own past like a dream. Correction, more like a nightmare. Your fear is your weakness, Ralph. And yet, your fear might protect you from danger.' Edwin was amazed at the Timeman's frankness. And he also detected malice in the Timeman's voice. He stared at his grandpa in disbelief. Suddenly, Mr Cougar's phantom disappeared. He was united.

'Let's see how your grandpa wants to overcome my reality. I hope he realizes that once in a while his higher level of consciousness comes in contact with his lower one. He won't have any experience of what he had seen with us.'

'I thought you said that my grandpa's emotions will be the cause of his own defeat. And you won't miss that chance to work on his weaknesses.'

'Know well the lord of time. Follow me very closely, but don't interrupt,' commanded the Timeman.

15:30 Cougar's Eye Hole

The head of Mr Cougar's bed was still slightly raised, and it seemed to wrap around him. Everyone was alarmed when he closed his eyes because they believed that a mysterious evil was taking control over him. The trance appeared to glue his eyelids together to hide the identity of a fearless opponent from others. Hidden from everyone, the silvery stream of light beam played off his pupils from which Mr Cougar's spirit floated into the room. And then it glanced at the helpless lump in his bed. Most spectators in his room were staring at his long gray hair and beard that covered part of his face and looked like a silver mushroom on his head. His spirit reentered into his body; and yet, it could not wake his body up. His subconscious entertained a bluish stream of light. He thought that the light was truly himself, and that he was identical to it. With this little speck that his body could nourish, he intended to do battle against his adversary, the Timeman.

A voice rang within him: 'Your dreadful destiny, you can't escape. Never! The unchangeable and the unmovable, I am. Before you the absolute stands. My scope and my greatness, your mind is too small to imagine. The worst thing for you is me, eating away inside of you eternally.'

'You're so powerful. And still, you want to torture an insignificant person like me,' thought Mr Cougar subconsciously. And he waited for the Timeman to say something unpleasant.

'Your primitive sensations in any realms; obey my will. Without me your experience of joy, pain, and growing old couldn't be. Neither your thoughts nor your reality, can escape me. Yes, the measure of all, I am. In every motion and change, my mystery works,' boasted the Timeman.

Mr Cougar struggled with the thought of why he had to confront this repulsive and annoying monster. This, he wanted to reconcile in himself. For sure, he did not know very much about himself. This made him believe that his destiny had to be written down somewhere. Naïve of his own nature, he had renewed a deep thirst in himself to have the whole picture of his life. But the Timeman stood before his thoughts like an impenetrable barrier; it was tormenting him; Mr Cougar could not run away and hide from the Timeman. With all this in mind, he had no choice; he finally accepted that he had to be humble before the most undesirable and ill-defined creature in the universe:

'Yes, you're what we called "time." You've given humans, animals, fishes, insects, plants, illusions of growing, multiplying, dying, and nourishing each other, thought Mr Cougar. But Ralph Cougar isn't an illusion! You may own my body, work magic with it, gobble it up. Crispy skin to remind me of swimming. Exhibit me like a clown. Make me the most horrible creature among my friends. Torment me as much as you want, and still your most awesome horror doesn't scare me. Nothing could change the Cougar in me' it's timeless!' As he was waiting for the Timeman's reply, his subconscious looked into the past for some answers about himself. Coming empty handed from his self-introspection, his subconscious prepared itself for a furious storm ahead.

'Thinner than a shadow, you are! Your own fictitious whim of my essence of greatness, you enjoy. A shallow fool, you are. Behold, the truth, worst misfortune awaits your fossilized sentiments. All your sentiments—ideas, inspiration, wisdom, virtue—belong to my realm of time. One after another, all things lifelessly await to be strung up. Outside of my domain, there isn't anything.'

'Timeman, what do I know of your nature?' Cougar asked.

'Whatever you wish me to be, I am. Without me, your daily life is impossible. To string all your experiences together as before and after couldn't be done without me. Your entire life history, before and after, I nicely pack for you. Around me, are all your activities. You joyfully think of me as one-dimensional. Time flowing continuously and regularly to the past is how you see me. How much you believe what your clock measures on the wall is identical to my nature. Look how the second hand is ticking away—tick-tock-tick-tock. Tick-tock—the future is here. Tick-tock, the present slips to the past,' he smiled sarcastically, because Mr Cougar could not escape him.

'I knew it all along, you're time – past, present, and future,' he thought as though he had won the battle against the Timeman because everything would finish at four o'clock. 'Yes, without time, I couldn't organize my life. I wake up at five in the morning. Breakfast at seven o'clock. I see a few friends before midday. Then dinner. I go to the store before it closes in the afternoon. And then supper comes. I look at a few television programs until I go to bed. If there wasn't any time, my life would be chaotic.'

'Stepping out from the flow of time, you can't. A holiday away from me, you can't take either. How beautifully your ignorance blossoms about my nature!'

'Ignorance is a blessing not bliss.'

'Tell your father's grandparents, the Cougars' heritage that! All the Cougars before you, I've strung in my net. None could escape my destiny. Powerlessly, your father's grandparents looked at the tide coming in and going out. Before me, they humble. They could pop up any time and help you, don't you think? All existence, wears my stamp. Yes, the world of the dead, I roam over, too. Everything you feel, think, touch, taste, see, imagine, and dream: my imprint, they all have. All of them, even a rock, believe in me. Through me, everything has its place. Proud, I may be. And proud I should be, for all originate for me.'

'My grandparents are prisoners in your domain! How could this be?'

'You, Cougar-child, have inherited their sad faith, too. Don't think the ghosts of your ancestors could manifest themselves and help you to escape me! And you, don't you believe that a person could be abolished from all realms. At my disposal, you exist. Life and death, obey me!'

'My grandparents, who are they? What does all this have to do with me?' he interrogated himself, for it was apparent that he was suffering from his grandparents' deeds.

'Your father's ancestors, it must be clear in your feeble mind. Their barrier to mingle in the past and peep into the future, I've removed. How powerful they are to you, but useless for me! At will, I could abolish their freedom. Only me dictate all the worlds to be and those that had already gone.'

Mr Cougar wanted to talk about his reoccurring dreams of the terror of the sea and the terror of under-the-sea meeting. 'Right now, my body obeys your awful wickedness. But my mind is becoming ripe to overcome your bondage forever. My mind is taking in energy from all my dear friends and families to confront you,' he thought.

'Restrictions and limit, none I have. Under every stone, you'll find me. And yet, I'm not there in my essence!'

'Why torment me, a poor soul? I couldn't harm a fly. Whose penalties am I suffering?' Cougar waited. No answer came. Suddenly, images were slowly becoming clear in his mind and he entertained them verbally.

'A dark night in a ship. The ocean is calm, too. What am I doing here? Look, a figure is coming from the crew's cabin. Could it be a man? Yes, he is! And he's coming toward me. What? He's walking too rigid, like a ghost. Yes, he couldn't be sleepwalking. He has his blue and white pajama and cabin shoes on. He's getting closer to me. What should I say to him? Oh, no! He walks right past me! Not even saying a word to me. What is the matter with him? Couldn't he see me standing right near him? He's so young with blonde hair. That face! It looks familiar. But who is he anyway? He doesn't even turn back. I'll run ahead and stop him. Oh, ho! Hi! He can't hear me. Yes, I should block his way. What? This can't be! He walks right through me like I'm smoke. He's climbing the narrow stairs. Oh, he wants to go to the deck. I guess some fresh air will do him good. Hello! Do you see me? Hello, hello! Wake up, will you? He has to be a sleepwalker! Or, could he be dead? Dead or alive, I've to stop him. He shouldn't do this on a ship. It's too dangerous. Hello! Wake up before it's too late! Why doesn't he hear me? I have to stop him.

Yes, take him by his pajamas, that should work! Come back here! What? All of my strength is so useless. He's still walking away from me. But where is he going?. Strange, he doesn't walk into anything on the deck. Something must be wrong with him. Why doesn't the fresh cool air wake him up?

'I think I hear something. What is that? A voice, it's calling. At this time of the night! Something funny is happening here. But what is it? I can't see anybody else on the deck? But who is calling him? Listen, it's calling again! Why is it calling him? It's coming from the water. I have to take a quick look. I might see it. Nothing! *Sicitur adastra*, he's climbing over the side. Run, run! Faster and faster, before it's too late! Darn, overboard! Why did he do it?

'I have to save him! I have to jump in after him. Yahoo! How come I can't feel the freezing water? Forget the water, where is he? Maybe he doesn't know how to swim? Yes, he should be around here. I've got to help him! But where is he?

'Look! I see him, now. He's sinking – deeper and deeper to the ocean bed. Yes, I grab his hand. Pull, pull harder! Why couldn't I bring him up? He's still sinking. I've to save him. It's so dark down here. I've to save him before it's too late. What's that? It's pointing a red light at us in this black pit. It's to be a submarine coming. Yes, somebody is coming to help him! But a submarine couldn't come straight up with such a great speed? Who cares! Finally, help is coming. Oh, no! It isn't a submarine! Nothing could be at this depth. This water pressure would crush it like biscuits! It couldn't travel that fast either. Who cares, he'll be saved now, and that's important.

'Oops! It's a shark, over forty meters long! *Sicitur adastra*, it swallows both of us, head first. What's going on? It doesn't want to eat us yet! Why does it keep us in its mouth?

'I have to wake him up, but he isn't waking up. I can't even move him. How can we escape now? He can't even move! What? It's taking us up straight to the surface at lightning speed. Why doesn't it swallow us? Chewing us up with those razor sharp teeth? But no, it just holds us in its huge mouth. It's getting a bit bright in here. But its mouth is still closed. No, it's open a bit. At least, there isn't any water in here.

'Why isn't it slimy? Oh, yes, I should have known this. Salt water wastes it away. But where is it taking us now? It's strange! Oh, no! It's moving him to its throat! Now it'd swallow him whole! Holy, *sicitur adastra*! What should I do? We stop moving in its throat. But why? Its gills are opening wider. I can feel cool air coming in from somewhere. What's all this? How could this be? A shark is helping me to save him. It's unbelievable!

'What? Are those stars I'm seeing? They are. I can walk in its mouth. Sit around anywhere, even sleep in it. But where is it taking us? Doesn't it get tired swimming so fast over the splashing waves? I shouldn't think so much about the shark, only about this young man. It's hard to see his face in the night. Holy, *sicitur adastra*, I can feel his heart beating! He isn't dead!

'Oh, it's morning already! We're saved. What's that coming up from its throat? Slime and pieces of fish. Is it vomiting? Oh, it stinks in here! I better close this young man's mouth. This poison could kill anybody. But I can't, it's stuck open. He's floating with his mouth open in this rotten slime. It stops pushing up rotten fishes. It's swallowing it back. Where is it taking him? I'll be with you. And I'll save you from this monster. What? It's evening already! Have faith lad, you gonna be rescued. It's getting dark again. But we're still moving at the same speed. More slime coming up. Oh, yes! I get it. It's feeding him. Eat lad. It's the best food for your health. Eat!'

Suddenly, the scene disappeared; Mr Cougar waited for the outcome of his effort.

'Cougar-child! Your destiny, the terror of the deep was foreseen. Yes, healthier than all the kings it fed you. For eight days, your half dead body ate. Over nine thousand kilometers to spit you out here, your secret guardian traveled. Fishermen's curiosity heightened, when they thought they'd seen a capsized boat in the water. Like a storm they hurried to revitalize you. To Sandreef your incomprehensible and fathomless blackness, brought you. Even with this dark force on your side, you couldn't take me on!'

'I'll go away from your likeness with dignity, love, and humility,' he subconsciously thought.

155

'An imbecile, you are! Nothing about your nature, you've known.'

'I won't do any battle with you, Timeman. My death is written in me. Nobody's gonna stop that!'

'The most dishonorable, you are! Your ancestors, you've mindlessly betrayed. Then, too young for the sword and axe, you were. Their honor, your death in the ocean would have saved. Your kind, they don't want now.'

'My Ancestors, I don't have any ancestors. I don't want to carry any ancestral banners. I'm free from ancient obligation.'

'Fool again, life without any mystery in it is meaningless. You, nobody would look at! A pure blood Norseman, your father was! The honor of his roots, he wore bravely. To you, let the sea of your father come forth!' the Timeman commanded.

At a distance, Mr Cougar saw a little flame; it was pulling him onward. The flame got bigger and bigger as he got closer to it. The flame carved out axes and swords and engraved them with courage, bravery, and fearlessness. 'Our God, we've changed. Our soul sleeps in the ocean,' howled a Norse's voice in the flame. It rang in his ears like a bad dream. Then the flame blew him away to another dimension.

'Oh, I'm swimming among the clouds. I can see something down there. Yes, it's a ship. It's stuck in the Arctic ice. It's a fishing trailer. Its net got stuck on some moving ice. Other huge sheets of ice are moving in, around the ship. They'd crush the ship to pieces. Oh, I've to help—warn the captain! No, don't stop the engine! Why does he have to turn it off? Leave the net! Can't you see the mountains of ices moving in around you? It'll crush you. Start the engine and go! Oh, don't worry about your net, just go! I'll do it for you. I can't turn the switch on. Look captain! Can't you see the ice moving under the ship! It's taking the net with it. That's good. You see how it's pulling the ship with it. So, let the net go. Cut it! No, don't start the engine now! Holy, *sicitur adastra*, the blades would rip the net to thread around the ship's fan. You see, the engine can't turn now. You're going to freeze without any heat. Don't worry about the freezing cold outside. If you stay in the ship, you'll be crushed. Look at the mountains of ices coming around you!

'Who is that running on the deck without any shirt and screaming likes a wild beast? He's so tall and muscular like a giant. He couldn't be more than twenty-five years old. Why is he going haywire? Too scared, I guess.

'Wait a minute! He couldn't be my father. Could he? But I'm a skinny midget. Look at him, over a hundred kilo of muscles. His face, yes! It sings out fury, bravery, and courage. The same kind of eternal flame burns in his green eyes.'

'Your father, he is,' cried the Timeman.

'My father! I have to stop him before it's too late. Hello, hello Dad! Stop running and shouting like that. Why are you going to the captain's cabin? Oh, no! He takes the captain's double edge sword. Put it back before you hurt someone! Don't jump overboard! I've to go after him. Don't try to free the fan, leave it! Get back to the ship. Oh, he can't hear me. Cut then, faster and faster. Go up now, the ice is closing in. Go up! Leave it before it's too late. Go, go! It's finished. The fan is free. Yes, that's the spirit. You can make a hole through the ice. Yes, keep on swinging that sword. Please don't stop and stare at me like that. Dad, I'm your own son. You know me, Dad. It's me, Ralph, your loving son! Please dig! Why is your skin turning pink? This can't be.'

'Helping him, you can't. A ship in desperate distress, he saved. Stronger than more than fifteen men, your father, Eric Telford, was. His burning rage, your ancestors joyfully praised. The last from the noble tradition—the Old Norse, roaming the water as the most vicious predators on legs, they were. Your father's hands, you couldn't hold. Before the final stroke to shatter the wall of ice above him. Your coming, he saw. Dishonor of the proud throne, he saw. Without the eternal flame in your eyes, your father took the honorable sword with him. Brave as he was, the deep took him away. Broken hearted, he died!'

'My father's grandparents were Vikings.'

'Correction! Noble Old Norse,' replied the Timeman, and then he started to speak about the Old Norse who took up their residency in

Scandinavian countries were misleadingly called Vikings. 'The dark force of the oceans used to manifest itself in the form of any sea creatures and then guided the Old Norse across oceans. The Old Norse visited every shore and left artifacts there. In every place, they were known as Vikings.'

'You meant they raped all lands and shores in Europe and Asia. Their name was inscribed in every coastal village and city as savages. I've dreamt about the terror of the sea. Now, it's my father's bloodline. And I don't think that the Vikings have a proud past. They were murderers and rapists. They couldn't die warrior's deaths.'

Then the Timeman interrupted Mr Cougar's subconscious thoughts: 'The Old Norse weren't about the legion of drinking, robbing each other, cruelty, murders, and the strongest warrior in a tribe becoming leader. All this amounts to nothing. The legion is about the Old Norse who was ordained to retrace the route of the Older Norse. That custom was interrupted when the white God was born. The Christian God, Jesus Christ, fought against their dark gods. All that war took place within every Old Norse's heart. It was a long and bitter one. It drove every Old Norse mad. Because of this, they became the terror of humanity. The white God eventually won.

'Before the battle of the white God, the Old Norse was a threat to gods not man. They were known as the people who changed their gods at will. If a god did not give them success, they would take up another one to worship. Every four hundred years or so, they worshipped another god. On several occasions, they had changed their generous gods because they just felt like worshiping another one.'

'All this Old Norse stuff doesn't have anything to do with me,' Mr Cougar thought. This made the Timeman reveal some more of Mr Cougar's inheritance.

'In everyone's veins for nine thousand and eleven years, the Old Norse reigned. Four thousand years before the white cosmopolitan religion was born, the seas cherished the Old Norse's customs and rites. Sea friary was their altar. The Cult of Odin and the Gothic Dance, you've heard about. Their warrior god, Odin was. Only bersekers were Odin's people. But the truth is that the ancients invented Odin as an explanation for the bersekers. The last of the berseker's descendant, your father was. The destiny of a warrior, he carried with him. Like the dark rolling waves under the bersekers' boat, their gods were. To the ancestral route—the birthplace—the Old Norse lived for. Over seventeen hundred years to cultivate and to harvest its crop, the white God took. Like all fields, the unwanted also grew - your father.'

'I'm Ralph Cougar, not a Viking! I've nothing in common with barbarians, murderers, stupid brutes, plunderers, rapists, and drunkards. I don't steal other men's wives and daughters. I don't butcher people indiscriminately. Oh, no! I'm not warlike, I don't want to hear about the gods of the North men, especially, this "bare-sark".'

'Your father's medallion, you haven't seen? The ancient inscription of the berserker on it. To Edwin this morning, you thought that you'd passed it on to. Remember? The next inheritor, the medallion chooses by itself.'

Mr Cougar remembered that the history of the Viking era, from 700 to 1100 AD speaks about their craftsmanship, marine technology, exploration, and commerce. They were traders, not raiders, and freebooters swarming out of the northlands to burn and pillage Europe. He thought that he had dreamt about his own nature: the terror of the sea and the terror under the sea. Perhaps, the Timeman saw his destiny like an empty picture without any traces. And yet, his mind could not unravel why the Timeman was not angry with him anymore, and that he has never heard anything about the berserker people before.

'Berserkers, your ancestors were. Magically immune from all weapons. Shape-shifters, they were too. Changing their form to bears, wolves, birds, sharks, and fishes. Possessors of furious qualities, war fury and rage burned in their eyes. True warriors, they were. Running into battle without any armors, these murderous savages went. With their ferocity and acquired strength of bears or wolves, fear killed their enemies. The most vicious predators on two legs, they were the terror of the sea.

'Conquerors and kings of the Vikings, they weren't. And yet, in every battle and conquering expedition, their names were carved. Fury and burning rage, the berserk people were to the Viking Age. Every shore from their forefathers, the berserker knew. To have their temple at sea, to retrace their father's route, and to go to their god—the depth of the sea after death: was their destiny. To the Caspian Sea, China, India, Russia, Asia, Middle East, Europe, South America, and North America, they migrated. A direct inheritor of the Old Norse, the berserk, you are. The Viking era of the North Sea, you have.

'Ordained with Draugr, the walking dead, the berserkers were. Once their dead body was put in a grave, a strange life and power they had. A pseudo-life within the grave like a ghost, they lived. Mound-dwellers or after-goers, the dead body living on, they were. The most terrifying, their undead corpse was. Swell to enormous size, become extremely heavy, change its shape to any forms—a seal, a shark, or a wolf—it could. Magical power to see the future, to swim through the earth and solid stone, draugr possessed. At sea, the berserkers buried their dead. The guiding stars of the living sea-berserks, they became.'

The voice took a short break in his head; Mr Cougar waited for some more. He thought that now he has known his Norse's history about the berserkers' roles in Viking society. Besides superior warriors to the king's armies and protectors of royal powers, they were a predatory group of killers of other Viking communities. He was frightened by that picture of terror. Then he compensated himself by treasuring the idea of the white God who brought about a civilized central Europe and overcame the Norsemen. With a slight hesitation, he recollected that the Timeman had told him that nearly all the berserkers mingled with the white God, but a few remaining ones kept the fury and rage burning inside. 'So, I'm an Old Norse. I inherit the berserkers' destiny. And, I couldn't die, because berserkers are also draugr. I'll be a ghost! No, I'll die. I want to die!' he cried subconsciously.

'All, you've missed. You, your Norse ancestors had disowned, unworthy of being among them. What they'd seen, you hear me out well. That night of your falling overboard, my name in the wind your berserker forefathers sang out. No physical strength to change the future, Berserkers have today. Their enchantment, I answered. Another one in my grasp just like your grandparents, you'd have been restored. Yes, as my royal spectators to wander in the past, present, and future, I kept your ancestors alive with. Meaningless wandering through time they could do freely. To change anything, they're powerless. My reality, they couldn't escape. The Old Norse called, I heeded at once. Your berserker's name, I sang to you while you were sinking to the ocean bed. Then beyond my domain, you sank. To the darkest depth of the ocean bed, you were out of my reach. You, I waited for…. But the dark force intervened in the form of a shark. For days and nights beside the blackest force, I waited for you. What's ordained in my domain, you can't escape. The future, your mother couldn't change.'

'My mother! She must be more powerful than you are. She broke your plan.'

'Your real mother, you don't know. Esmeralda, isn't your mother. After your real mother died, she'd softened you up. Then, death should have been your destiny.'

'What, Esmeralda isn't my mother? Who is then?'

'That medium coming between your eyes held the truth.' Suddenly, Mr Cougar's subconsciousness was sucked up by an approaching circular hole. 'A realm beyond my time, you'll witness.'

'*Sicitur adastra*! What an incomprehensible place to see, greenish-bluish cloudy waves everywhere. No horizon, no corners, edges, and no up or down. It has no features or limit to it. I feel like I'm becoming it. Or, could it be that everything in it is becoming me? I'm everywhere, and everywhere is in me. My senses reach out endlessly. I better leave this infinite domain before it's too late. Where is the Timeman when you need him? Please get me out of here! Yes, the opening from which I came in is reopening. Hurry, but I can't move. Wait a minute, I'm getting smaller and smaller. This place is pushing me out through that hole. Thanks. *Sicitur adastra*, I made it out. It's safer from here. I could just look from this hole. Why do I feel like I've given myself a human form because it's the only thing I could slightly understand? My mind couldn't handle that infinite realm.

'Look, the greenish-bluish cloudy waves forming a shape for me to see. It's the smallest one for me to grasp. And still it's a gigantic oyster. My mind is too small to take in all this. This is unbelievable, the oyster is really bigger than anything I could ever imagine. A silvery foam is showing. I guess it's opening its clamps. Everything is so foamy, now. The foam is changing to a human. It's making itself the smallest for me to see as a figure. The figure is getting closer to me. *Sicitur adastra*, it's a woman in a blue-green silk dress. Her entire surrounding becomes the color of her dress. On her head is a golden crown with all sorts of precious stones on it. All around it are golden chains hanging. They reach her breast. On each chain, there's a circular pendant hanging like the one I had. All these gold chains hide her eyes, face, and hair. She has a pair of golden gloves on. Her silk dress covers her feet. She must be the queen around here. I think she sees me. What? More people are forming from her silk dress. Except for her golden crown, they even dress like her. They have long golden hair. But I can't see their faces. The Queen is slowly moving away from me. I think she drops something, one of her chains…. Her people are synchronizing themselves with her movement. The silk clothes behind her people are changing to golden ropes. Except for the queen, each of them holds an end of a rope with both hands. They are carrying the rope over their shoulders, as though they're going to pull something very heavy. The ropes are getting stiffer, completely stiff now. They're moving forward. But what is it tied to?

'Timeman, why are they pulling those ropes? Where are you? *Sicitur adastra*, they're peeling their own dimension away. It's like taking an old carpet away. Maybe the ropes are tied to the end of the greenish-bluish waves. Now they're turning it over. No, rolling it over. But why? Everything is changing in here so quickly. Are those stars and planets I'm seeing? Yes, they are. One moment everything was greenish. Now, everything is getting brighter. That's the blue sky, the clouds, and the ocean. Where are the queen and her people? They've disappeared. What? Did they roll themselves out of existence? Maybe they got themselves trapped in the thing they were pulling off. Oh, forget them. The water looks so warm and blue.

'What is that in the water? Could it be a tree in the ocean? Yes, it is, a tree in the middle of nowhere! There's something on that branch. What is that? No, it couldn't be, a little child on it. Why is he crying? Oh, he's such a tiny baby, all nude, except for his golden chain around his neck. He must be very cold and hungry. I' have to help him. *Sicitur adastra!* He isn't a boy, not a girl either. Who cares? I' have to help him! I should get him down from that high branch. Only water all around, but why? Oh, this poor child is all alone. I have to save him. The blazing sun on his back isn't good for him. But I'm so powerless, I can't do anything. I can't even comfort him. I'm like a ghost. Hi! Is everything OK? I'm here. Don't be scared. Oh, what is this? I'm holding his hands, but he can't feel me. I'm speaking to him, but I don't know whether he can hear me or not. Poor child, he's crying more and more. Please, don't cry. I'm here with you.

'This can't be! The more he cries the bigger he gets. And the water is receding from under the tree. I can see the ground now. It's a strange child, I must say. Look out! The branch is breaking. Darn, it's too late! He's on the ground. I hope he didn't hurt himself. Look how he is still holding onto that branch. Why doesn't he look up at me? He's at adult size now. *Sicitur adastra*, he just splits himself, in two halves—one half male has the golden chain on, and the other female. What, each half is becoming round again like before. Oh, I can't take this anymore.'

'Creation, you've just seen. A wonderful experience, it is. Not a name, the Goddess of creation has. All perfect, she was like all other gods and goddesses in their own ways. Perfection doesn't need time and space. Nothing physical, it needs. No time and space, her realm has. Her entire realm, she was. Then her realm, she took it with her.'

'Only in stories, I heard about this realm. Without you, I couldn't have seen able to see it for myself. My creator, I've seen.'

'In thought, the Goddess had conceived a child. Because this meant imperfection of seeing her seed, she left with her realm. The other realm was born with her child in our reality, as they were leaving. The birth of light, the child, and me were fused together. In essence, we were all molded together. Inseparable, we were.

'Nothing until now, the number 9011 meant to you. Our essence, it calls forth. It doesn't only mean the birth of the universe, Ralph! In due course, you'll know more about it.' Mr Cougar remarked that the Timeman's mood seemed to have changed more toward him. Finally, the confrontation between them appeared to be over. And he thought that the tree was the symbol of life. It kept the goddess' child alive.

'Yes, everything started around the Philippine islands, near the Tropic of Cancer. The child you saw on the tree was Ashram. Being the loneliest person in the universe, he wept. From crying, it grew quickly. And then he split himself. Pure love and harmony were born from it. Fear and loneliness were abolished from existence. The other half of Ashram is called Embla. Under that very tree, they separated from each other. Ashram went north. Embla took the Southern Hemisphere. Ashram was a hermaphrodite, and Embla too. Each of them could split only 9011 times. As Embla walked from one end of the Equator to another, she could split into any animals, trees, birds, fishes, plants… And each hermaphrodite animal would split to whatever it wished to be. Each hermaphrodite could split itself only 9011 times. Each animal or plant was a hermaphrodite. Embla was the goddess of the Southern Hemisphere. When these half-gods were living, they could roll off a hundred years in the future in a wink and get back at the same moment. Yes, there was no past, present, and future. They did not age either—just took on different sizes. An adult size animal could split to another adult. They only obeyed their internal nature to live harmoniously among their creations.

'On each shore that Ashram touched he gave life to another hermaphrodite. These Hermaphrodites were round like a bottle. Every living organism was a hermaphrodite. There were only love and harmony among all living things in the cosmos. Ashram journeyed to the northern seas, from Sea of Japan, Bering Sea, Beauport Sea,

Hudson's Bay, Gulf of Mexico, back to Newfoundland, Labrador Basin, Denmark Strait, Greenland Sea, Kara Sea, and to Norwegian Sea. Ashram lived permanently among the Scandinavia regions. He traveled to the Indian, Arctic, and Atlantic oceans and to his birthplace. He also journeyed often between the North Sea and Arabian Sea. Embla stayed in the pacific regions among the Philippine, Polynesian, and Hawaii islands. She mostly touched all the Pacific islands and Southern mainland.' The Timeman waited until Mr Cougar grasped the meaning of his life.

'Love and harmony couldn't sing out endlessly. These hermaphrodites were getting extremely powerful in their love. Their love song could be heard in other realms. It might have awakened the old gods. Perhaps, it did. Soon, my identity was gradually molding within each hermaphrodite. When it was mature enough, I took a drastic measure and separated myself from each hermaphrodite. Yes, I, the Timeman, was born. With my separation, all hermaphrodites were split in two, male and female. Coincidentally, both Ashram and Embla were in the process of having their last split. Embla's final split was a woman. She could only give birth to another female. This stopped with your birth. From Ashram's last split, only males were born until your father's birth.

'Ralph, my birth meant the end of immorality as you've known it. Death, sickness, suffering, pain, and broken hearts were born. Not only that, when I separated from each hermaphrodite, each half was left with the eternal task of searching for the other half. Yes, I'm the lord of all. I'm the essence of all things. And all is found in me. For 9,011 years after my separation, human beings had supernatural powers. Some had more powers in their domain than others. Yes, Ralph, that was the period of the Golden Age. As my power increased, the Golden Age slipped away to the Bronze Age. Greek Myth-makers spoke about how all hermaphrodites were separated and reduced to human beings. Each living person has a quest to rediscover love and harmony by finding the other half of himself. Even today, people search for true love and harmony. And they hope to find it in the other half. Unfortunately, when I separated myself from the hermaphrodite, I put one half a moment later from the other. If you compare any two persons, you'll observer that one of them is later than the other. For any persons, women or men, each of their internal clocks has been predetermined faster or slower. Even if you clone a million of them from a single person, each of them would have a different internal clock. Nine thousand and eleven marks all these changes in time.

'Nine thousand and eleven years after the splitting, the brute was born. Human beings created mythology to give themselves meaning, to explain how things come about, and how natural disasters and sickness came about. A New World of mythologies was born to account for death and life. Don't get me wrong, Ralph. The hope to find the other half still exists. But people get upset too quickly when they have to settle for the closest match. And yet, everyone has a time limit when searching for the other half of himself.'

'What happened to Ashram and Embla?'

'In the northern countries, Ashram lived and vanished in the process of populating half of the world. From the Golden Age until now, his children tried to retrace his route. They hope to bring back love and harmony in the world. At all costs to their own life or others', that journey had to be made. Now you see why they were the terror of the sea. They were foreordained to go back to their origin. Ralph, from this seed, your father comes from.

'Embla's people roamed as sharks in the south sea. Her offspring could roam to unknown depth. And yet, they were ordained to travel to her birthplace to bring back love and immorality in the world. Like Ashram, they fell short of it. They couldn't escape my realm of time. From Embla's seed, your mother comes.

'Your father and mother met accidentally in a fishing boat. That day in the Arctic Ocean when the fishing net got stuck. Your father went to the kitchen, for the first time in his life and he saw a woman cleaning the kitchen several meters away. As soon as their eyes reached each other's, you were conceived and born. Love was born and harmony sang at that moment. Pure love and harmony were too powerful for them. It drove them crazy. Your mother died while you were coming to the world. She left you alone. Her best friend brought you up like her own child. You were conceived from that love and harmony they had been seeking out. Ralph, you couldn't die.'

'I have to. And nothing will stop me from dying.'

'Impossible!' The Timeman echoed furiously. In the next instant, he shifted from anger to politeness: 'In the Bronze Age, every 911 years, your grandparents journeyed around the world. In 3600 BC, we had the great Indo-European migrations in Southern Asia and Europe. The Norsemen with boats heeded to the innate call to find Ashram's birthplace. During that period, urbanization had started in most countries. In 2700 BC, the Old Norse tried once again to find their roots. In 1800 BC, the Scandinavian tried as well. In 900 BC, other cultures started to follow the Norsemen home. Homer's *Odyssey* grew out of the Norse's quest. Nine hundred years later, the white God was born. But it didn't stop the quest. Nine hundred years after the birth of the white God, the Norsemen sailed around the world again, still without finding their home. This was the end of the Gothic Dance in European history. Then another period came alive: the cultural revolution of the industrial age.'

'You've told me everything about my Norse grandparents. But not so much about my mother!'

'Your mother, Ralph. She never heard her true name. How could she ever have known her inheritance? She was just a little kitchen girl. To the ship's captain, she was nothing more than a slave working for food. They called her "Hi Kay." A slave girl in a ship nobody wanted her. But this girl didn't know that she'd inherited Embla's destiny. She didn't know that she was destined to give birth to only girls, not boys. You must remember that they used to call you Vince on the fishing boat.

'Embla's kingdom was blossoming in 35,000 BC on an island around the Philippines when it sank. Fortunately, sharks transported her followers to several other islands. From that day on, Embla's people worshipped sharks—the terror under the sea. Your mother's birth name was Anathalia Freedman. She too had a quick funeral like your father. Perhaps, Embla caused her death instantaneously. Ralph, your birth is a curse to the terror under the sea. A male child is a curse in Embla's first born. The terror under the sea has also abandoned you, too.'

'Tell me more about my mother.'

'Anathalia was born in the Hawaii islands. She was a stowaway child on a fishing boat on its way to the Philippines. Esmeralda found her and brought her up like her own child. She brought you up, too. All your life, you thought she was your mother. Esmeralda told the captain of your mother's death. But she didn't tell him about a mysterious chain and pendant next to your mother. It came off your father. Esmeralda thought that she passed the chain on to you, her adopted son. However, the chain selected its next bearer. Ralph, your mother went out of this world the way she came in—unknown. The captain's unofficial report said that your father and mother died accidentally at sea.

'When your mother was giving birth, she was in a coma. She was witnessing her Embla's past. The enchantment of the deep still remains beyond the realm of time. They wanted your mother's death and your death, too. Because you couldn't inherit the throne. Somehow, your mother's inheritance saved you from dying and brought you here.'

'You meant to tell me that my life doesn't have any significance to anybody? Why wasn't I born a hermaphrodite? I'd have fused you into my nature.' Mr Cougar knew that the battle with the Timeman was not finished yet. He had to win.

'A traitor to the past, you are! Had it not been for your terror under the sea, in a box, you'd be packed for all time,' said the Timeman sternly.

'You're nothing! As far as I'm concerned, you're powerless. You can't change anything.'

'Knowing your inheritance doesn't make you strong enough to challenge me. Once, I came to claim you for your Norse's ancestor....'

'Don't be so sure of your victory, Timeman! Look at me, the terror of the deep combed me well. And maybe a little Viking flames still burns in me. My mind will be all the blades of the past! I don't care so much for any ancestral help. My mother's already had their victim. And the Norse has my father. Timeman, both worlds meet at me. Neither of them can strike me down without offending the other. They were looking for me. Now, they've found me. So, not even you know your own destiny, Timeman. '

'No, Ralph! None of them sees any honor in you. The deep never accepts a male as its inheritor. It prefers to be lost in annihilation than to have the likes of you. The image of the Old Norse, your father's seed, you could never wear. You've exterminated several thousand years of honors. You destroy the only dignity in their world. Now, they're weeping up storms and hurricanes. You've killed them. You've condemned them to the worst prosecution. Every single one of them is crying his heart out. Crying out to die a thousand deaths rather than witness and contend with your disgrace of wanting to die. Ralph, you're lost. Only to my faith and mercy, you're condemned to.'

Unconsciously, tears were running down Mr Cougar's cheeks; he was feeling completely unsure of himself. He had to disappoint his loving families, friends and every single human being. 'Who does the Timeman think he is? Is he real enough to inflict this pain, suffering, and guilt on me? I don't deserve all this. I thought that I was just a simple ordinary Joe. All this guilt and burden, I don't deserve.'

'Ralph, you still have eternal life like everybody else. Pick out the strongest impression of your life. It could be something pleasant or something terribly awful. What would it be? Seeing your first-born came in the world, swimming with Edwin, taking your Marina's hand in marriage, fishing, swimming with sharks, or the golden sand under your feet. All this surprises you, doesn't it? You can't rank your most important image in your life, can you? Yes, give me an impression of your past, and you'll experience that image eternally. Day-in-and-day-out, twenty-four hours a day, seven days a week, for all time. You'd live in that image over and over again. You couldn't escape the magic of what eternal life is. Ralph, this is paradise. Living eternally with the last image in your mind before your physical death. I offer you the glory of eternal paradise like the white God does.'

'Even if my Norse grandparents didn't call your name out, you'd have still been here, wouldn't you? I was conceived in pure love and harmony. I'm here to restore people's burning love and harmony. Isn't that so, Timeman?'

'Your dreadful destiny, you couldn't escape. Before the like of you, the unchangeable and unmovable, I proudly stand. My greatness, you can't imagine. You don't have a place without me. Your blunt sensation of living can't pass my realm. Your daily life can't infect my essence. Because of time, all things have an identity and essence. Without me, you can't understand becoming old and the changes from an acorn to an oak tree.'

'How could you be so rude and compassionate at the same time? This isn't normal,' Mr Cougar subconsciously questioned.

'Ralph, you ask for my symphony of colors. How I vibrate to all spine and spineless creatures alike. How I string everything tightly together for love to work over. And yet, your primitive mind can't grasp what is elusive and imperishable at the same time. No mysteries, I have. Can you conceive how I'm in all things; and yet, I'm in none of them at the same time?

'Do you grasp how the clock on your wall is ticking? It reminds you of life ticking away like a faded line. Yes, time is real for you, isn't it? With time, you understand how an oak tree comes about. How you've changed from a child to a senile adult. And your fruitless and combative ordeal with me is hopeless! In your daily life, you can't make me any more real than your miserable aggregated composition—you call Ralph. All of your activities are arranged, planned, programmed, and scheduled around me—time. Look at your fishing community. They synchronize their alarm clock with the early tide at four. At five they're on the dock. At six they're pulling in their catch. Eight o'clock in the morning, they return and eat breakfast. Just before ten, they've already sorted out their harvest. After that, they just sit about until twelve o'clock for the fishing truck. For you, they can't organize their life without me. Not at all, the tide obeys me, too.

'That isn't all, I'm more real than you can imagine. Your personal history is a collection of events strung together by time. You recall your past as a sequence of experiences, before and after, don't you? Time works in you in a mysterious way. Your entire life experience becomes sensible because of me. If I were truly mean to you, I'd have removed myself from your well-packed life. Then you'd be rushed to the nearest madhouse for treatments. Without me, you wouldn't have a past. Until now, I haven't disappointed a single soul. I stretch myself in a unidimentional direction, a linear flow from the future to the past. How continuous, am I? Everybody packs the future as untouchable and unknowable. Oh, yes! That's how I protect everyone from themselves.

'You may think that I flow to an infinite past. And at the same time, you don't think of me as having an infinite coming. Does it occur to you that I can't be the future or the past of myself. Know this well: only one thing is permanent, imperishable, and indestructible—it's me! All physical things become, change, and perish, but not me. Can you comprehend that I'm in all things? And yet, I'm not in anything. Yes, all living things record their experiences as earlier and later, before and after. You've recorded Betty's birth before Catherine', haven't you? Yes, mental events register physical events in the world. If you want to see the world as everything being relational, you're still in my domain.'

'How boring and lifeless time is! We do much more than merely organize and plan our lives like a bus timetable. We want to step aside from it sometimes.'

'Only one manifestation of my realm you've seen so far, and you think that you could abolish me out of existence. Wrong again, Ralph! How many times do I have to tell you that I made all things free by splitting them in half. Until this day, none of them has found the perfect match. Each half is set a few moments apart. Look at any married couple: one partner is either sooner or later. They struggle to be on the same wavelength. They can't dance to the harmony of time. You still believe in Platonic love, but you refuse to see my reality. Look at yourself! How perplexed, you are! You accept the difference between sooner and later. But you don't admit that for some people, you might appear to be sooner. And for others, you seem later. You doubt how people see things differently. Let me remind you of your fictitious reality.'

'You miserable snake! You took away our harmony, and our love for each other. How could you do such a hideous thing to us?'

'Because of this, you want to die, don't you? But you can't! Remember, both of your parents died from it.'

'Are you telling me I'm hopeless against hearing about your boring nature?'

'You aren't dried up like a sand hill, yet! Pleasure, pain, anxiety, nervousness, and boringness—all of them I pour into you. You can't remember how many times you experienced me as shorter and longer. When you were waiting for Marina in the delivery room. Five minutes seemed like an hour to you. Waiting for your first-born was unbearable. Your shoes' tracks on the hospital floor showed your anxiety and nervousness. A minute was gruesomely torturing. The pain gradually intensified, and the clock appeared to have stopped for you. After the climax, you couldn't believe it. You had your own seed in your hand. You couldn't imagine a human being could be so little and perfect. Tiny fingers and toes were working perfectly and harmoniously. You were overwhelmed by the wonder before you. You believed that you knew the secret of life by just looking at the baby in your hands. Three hours slipped away without you noticing it. That short-lived happiness and joy was nothing compared to true happiness and love. But again, to affirm that there's a truth is to deny my existence. But you can't get to the truth without me, so you're doomed!'

'Those three hours were pure happiness. And you don't exist for me, Timeman!'

'Ralph, I'm showing you how I work in everyone's heart. Everybody experiences me psychologically. Each person's psychological clock beats at a different speed, too. How thoughtful I'm to separate one person from another psychologically.

'My mind clock separates everyone mentally. It makes a person either sooner or later from another. The Timeman needs entertainment, too. I can read your thoughts much more precisely than you can.

Now, you're thinking of synchronizing two clocks. And both of them would measure time exactly alike. Now, you're thinking about synchronized dancing. Dancers are waving their hands and jumping around at the same time. You think that there's harmony when people perform the same action at the same time. Ralph, I expect much better from you. Starting any two things at the same time is a principle, and starting two clocks to measure the same time is an impossibility. In the universe, you can't find two identical events. And worse, each thing has several internal clocks. All of them work at different rates. You can see for yourself how a thing can't be at the same place at two different times. It's an illusion.'

'Come to think about it, I believe I know you intuitively,' Mr Cougar entertained in his subconscious. 'You pass on to us your identity. Maybe I've an innate concept of you. And yet, you still remain illusive to me. I believe that all living things have innate ideas of your reality. If you're really the Timeman, you allow us to know you. So you can be known.'

'How amazingly wonderful you are! You think that everybody has an intuitive idea of my nature. Beyond order and regularity, you want to go. When the goddess created all things in the universe, she made everything knowable for animals with the slightest intelligence. Animals don't care about how the universe works. And they don't search for an intuitive understanding of reality. Their intuition and instincts are fused together to make them adaptable to their environment. On the other hand, humans have beliefs about her wonders and accomplishment. Look into your own mind. Do you see how you stretch yourself to capture an intelligent explanation of creation? And yet, the truth of my nature remains deceptive to everyone. I don't have any physical qualities and attributes. I'm like one of your bouncing balls. I always come back to myself, and nobody can escape my bouncing nature. Humans try to separate their instincts from their innate ideas in their daily lives, and this makes the intuition of time float around without any owner. So, Ralph, don't speak to me about human intuition. Intuition doesn't have any particular owner. It belongs to nobody.'

'If I get you right, you're telling me it's impossible to know you. After four today, I won't be here. You get it?' He felt a bit happy. But he did not at the moment realize that his thought was transparent for the Timeman, and he could not dispel of him so easily.

'Poor fool! You're no threat to me. Have you forgotten how childish you are compared to me? To make matters worse for you, all languages obey the realm of time, or else you'd be babbling meaninglessly. I bounce around in your grammar. The future, present, and past couldn't be sensible without time. Look and listen, Ralph! Do you hear that young man's thought? The one who is sitting at his desk and looking at his agenda? You see how he plans his tomorrows?' Mr Cougar bitterly struggled to suppress the image of the man, and he could not help thinking that the Timeman was behaving like an inconsiderate spy of people's minds.

Mr Cougar attended to the man's thoughts: "At six tomorrow, I'm going to see a film, the film will have finished at eight. At eight thirty, I'll be meeting Susan...."

'How degrading of you to read someone else's mind,' thought Mr Cougar.

'Ralph, let's go to that expensive restaurant. Look how lovely and ravishing that young woman enchants the air around her. Have a better look inside her! See her rage and anger. Like a lightning bolt they're lashing out in her head. No, Ralph, her brain won't explode. Her emotions have an outlet. See how her body twisting and curling up like a furious storm sweeping away a coastal village. Love and tenderness can't charm and subdue a storm, but they can calm her emotions, yes.'

The Timeman showed him what the woman said to herself:

"Darn, I always have to wait for him. I've been waiting here for twenty minutes. My God, I always have to wait for him. I'm still waiting! How could I be so cruel to myself? I'll be waiting here until I'm gray. Oh, no, not me!" she thought sadly. Seeing her lover approaching, her heart had screamed out how special he was.

'Ralph, do you see how I manifest myself in your everyday reality?'

'You infect our lives too much!'

'Ralph, you're getting more and more spontaneous. Is this how you intend to place a barrier between both of us? Don't you want to check your own thoughts before speaking? Well, if you want to be a stranger to yourself, go ahead. Disown your own thoughts. Is this how you want to emancipate your thoughts from my slavery? But you want to reduce yourself to the level of a beast. Nothing could change the cyclical nature in all living organisms,' he provoked Mr Cougar.

'I can't reverse nature, but only my own destiny.'

'Never! See how I'm in all things! Do you feel the soft refreshing raindrops. Look, everywhere is muddy and wet. Underneath that loose soil, a little eye of an acorn is shooting out to become an oak tree. Every spring, I renew life on earth like this. Flower buds and new leaves spring up to greet the sun. Rosebuds to make life colorful and refreshing. The summer is just long enough to harvest its fruits. Then autumn rolls in. It prepares the old to pass away. Some stay back for the winter to preserve. Look at springtime in Montana! Bulls and cows are working out their internal clocks. Yes, Ralph, it's mating season. It's the copulation of the internal cyclical clock with the seasonal one. Yes, I know that certain animals' cyclical clocks are determined by food. Food abundance for pigs means being in heat more often. So you've more pigs to eat. Don't forget, food regulation can't escape the seasonal clock. You can't squeeze more food from a long and harsh winter, can you, Ralph?'

'Organisms have biological clocks, not seasonal clocks,' thought Mr Cougar, thinking that the Timeman could not be in all aspects of life as he professed to be.

'Wrong again! A sad case, you're making for yourself. Look at any biological clock. It can't tick without me. Sperms swim and struggle to reach the ovary first. All of them want to fuse themselves with an egg. You see that one over there, it'll reach first. It's the most powerful one. There you have it. See how fast germination takes place. Now, you see a human embryo taking shape. Don't try to close your mind! You'll miss all the little working clocks in a person:

the size clock, maturity clock, shape clock, food intake clock, the movement clock, in the fetus. Her head is finally down. She's waiting for her mother to push her out. That little girl is nothing more than a bundle of miniaturized clocks. There're only clocks from: fetus, childhood, puberty, adulthood, and middle adulthood to the golden age. All this you call the biological clock. In all these stages, in each person, there are more than a billion little clocks. In life, some clocks stop working while new ones come into existence. And some slower than others. Of all these clocks, I am the lord. A unity to life, I bring joyfully to you!'

'But all our clocks work harmoniously.'

'Harmony! What do you know about harmony? If that's what you called it, let's see how it works in you. Your heart beats sixty-two times per minute. The heart of a young man, you have. Your blood pressure is sixty-eight by one hundred and twenty, like an athlete. Normal bodily temperature, too. Other than that, you are aging one year every fifteen minutes. You're completely gray. Miraculously, you've more hair on your head now than you ever had. Your face, it only gets smoother and rounder. Your hands, feet, and stomach are like salt-fish in the sun. Your skin, if that what you want to call it, *is* nice and crisp. It'll break and peel off to the bone. With all the liquid they're pouring into you, it couldn't restore you. Your mind burning off all the liquid of your body. It'd never be ripe enough to defeat me. Until now, I haven't seen any harmony in you, Ralph. You look like a monster. Even your heart is beating without pumping anything.'

'You couldn't degrade me anymore. Exhibit me worst than a fish without water to my loved ones. I know one thing for certain. You can't change what is unchangeable. You can't win me over, Timeman!'

'Are you telling me you're living in the eternal now? You've no past or future. Only the present is real for you? And I can't touch you? Let me show you how to practice the existential now. See over there in the African desert? Look at that those people sitting on the hot sand. Their bodies should remind you of how you look. Look at their dried up skin and their long and narrow jaws. They're practicing the eternal now. Only the present is real for them. Neither the future nor the past exists. Their empty stomachs and dry throats grumble for their god. They don't have much blood left in their veins to give their children a sip. In their eyes you can't see any future. And their past is untouchable like their future. Don't they all look meaningless and lost to you? It makes you wonder what still keeps them alive, doesn't it?

'You've seen enough of my beautiful vibrations in all things. No beginning and no end, I have. The flowing of time is an appearance of myself, but you can't get to the real me. Ralph, would you like to be locked up in your own thoughts eternally? Can you live in a single idea or image eternally? Heaven or hell is the consequence of the last thought or image of a dying person, Ralph. And a dying person holds onto the strongest impression in his mind before death. After he has passed away, he becomes a prisoner of that thought for all eternity. All of your Viking ancestors are locked up in seeing their failures and a short unit of the future. What will it be for you?'

'A simple death.'

'That can't be found anywhere! There isn't any death for you.'

The Timeman looked at Mr Cougar's thoughts about Marina in her dying bed. Her last remark reoccurred to him: "If you hadn't been a man, I wouldn't have married you. I couldn't have lived with you for so long." Then the image of Hercules as a powerless man interrupted the image of his wife. Hercules was waiting in front of the Golden Gate for his father to reclaim him. In humility, he cried "O father of Olympia! I don't want to die a human death!"

'Yes, Hercules couldn't die as a man or as a god. He couldn't escape me. An ageless depressive case, he had become. All strength without any glory in his quest. Everything obeys me.'

Mr Cougar became at ease, as he saw his opponent as utterly invincible in all domains of existence – becoming and perishing. 'Ok, I get it. My thoughts and my language are also a product of your domain.'

'Ralph, I mold you up grain by grain. You wear my stamp. But look at yourself how you think about me. I'm the most horrible creature that nobody dares to confront in his path. Am I really the evil mother of all, a curse staring in from the window, a parasite to the living?'

'If this is my ultimate battle, I won't be the last one to challenge you!' thought Mr Cougar.

'You're my eternal slave. I'll seal you in your last thought for eternity.'

'Why don't you show me the future? Are you scared? You know that you can't defeat me.'

'The future you want to see. You don't even know how diverse the future could be. If that's what you want to see, then look here in the casino. You see that short man over there. He dresses causally. He's already lost his wages and his car. He had just traded the deed for his house to the charier for one hundred and fifteen thousand dollars. What an obsessive gambler he is? And yet, a very smart one. He always doubles his loss. He said to himself over and over again, that only once he wanted to win, and then he'd never gamble again. He speaks the language of obsession. Look carefully and see how he'll lose that forty thousand he put on number seven. How wide he opens his eyes! He's trying to hypnotize the spinning wheel and the little ball. You can hear how he's screaming inside himself for number seven to come. He can't believe it. He can't understand why the ball stops at number twenty-six.' They observed him, as the gambler gobbled up his double scotch and orders another one. Everyone around him sympathized with him, for they were all losing as well.

'Why don't you take your losses and go home?' thought Mr Cougar.

'Let's change his luck, Ralph. We have to go in his head and then give him the image of the future number to come. There, he goes again. His money is on number eleven. He thinks about shooting himself if he loses. He's very impatient, wouldn't you say? The wheel is spinning slower and slower. He doesn't want to look at it, so he empties his scotch glass. He's won! Look at his joy. He's in a shock. He doesn't know what he's doing anymore. He's going crazy.' Slowly the casino disappeared from Mr Cougar's subconscious.

'That's luck, not your influence.'

'Ralph, that young man lost everything a week ago. He went

home a broken person. His wife didn't know that she'd married a gambler. All this time she thought that he was having an extramarital affair. To make matters worse, see the outcome for yourself. Yes, she has a three-month-old baby in her hand. Their older little girl is sleeping. Her husband threw them out into the cold. She finally had the strength to leave him. Another broken family, Ralph. Look at the gambler! He drains the bottles at every cheap bar. Next week, he'll be fired from his job.

'Let's go back to the casino and change everything, Ralph. You see how he trades in his chips for cash. The cashier fills a plastic bag for him. All his winnings are in that bag. It isn't finished yet. His whole body is numb with joy. Yes, Ralph, I know he sings lousy. He's leaving the building and crossing the street. But he doesn't see that car coming. It'd take his life away in nine seconds, Ralph. Bang! He's dead instantly. His money flies all over the street. Passers-by are busy grabbing money rather than seeing whether he's still alive. He's been so obsessed about his winning that he couldn't attend to his body alerting him about the coming car.'

'How can you be so insensitive to a person's life like that?'

'You don't like the bang, dead on the spot. Ralph, it's too messy for you, isn't it? Let's give him another image of his coming accident!

'Instead of crossing the street for a taxi, he phones for one at the door. He conducts himself carefully. He doesn't want to go home straightaway. The taxi drops him off at a luxurious hotel. How smart he is to put most of his winnings in a safety deposit box at the hotel. Look at him in the bar, how he buys everyone a drink. Everybody surrounds him like a dear old friend. And he enjoys himself like a generous king. Look there! He didn't see a night prowler coming toward him. Oh, yes, she's very sexy. Any innocent person would prefer to loose faith than to accept the white God's kingdom. Look how gracefully she allows him to sweep her off her feet. The king shows his power to his commoners and rents an expensive suite for the night. He tells her his secret before he slumbers. Look Ralph, how quickly she puts one and one together and steals his safety deposit box key. She takes his winnings and disappears. You see my point,

Ralph? The gambler doesn't want a single glance into the future. And he needs an infinite number of glances into the future. You don't want to make his life a series of changing future events. If you turn a bolt in the future, all the other bolts have to be turned as well. To reap the benefit of a single glance into the future, a thousand other future events would have to be changed. Remember the woman who stole the gambler's money. See how she's driving nervously on the highway. She's changing lanes recklessly, bang right into another car! The driver of the other car loses control, and the red truck smashed into it, killing everyone inside, Ralph.'

'No!' his subconscious shouted internally. Immediately, he was thrown into consciousness. He opened his eyes with horror. Realizing his surroundings, he smiled at everybody, thinking that everyone heard him shouting. But he knew that they did not. He was feeling a bit content, but his greeting did not change his mourners' facial expressions very much. And yet, his eyes did not only show an unknown depth, but their honesty and simplicity stood out majestically from his silvery gray beard. He glanced briefly at the clock hanging on the wall and expressed a concise smiled for everyone to see. The clock had been the only thing in the room that showed external motion for him. Quickly he slipped back to his interrogation with the Timeman; it reoccurred to him as a monumental doubt concerning his own nature:

'Maybe, I'm not ready to die. I haven't suffered enough. My mother has to help me. I have to go to the deep, the pit of darkness. But why doesn't the Timeman speak about them? From darkness, I've originated. It must be the first existence, and then light follows. What am I talking about? It couldn't be the deep. Darkness is older than the Timeman's universe. It's true, isn't it? The terror of the deep must be greater than the Timeman's rigid domain. But why does he want me to be trapped in his reality. But again, there's no way out.

'Am I condemned in the arena of timeless agony and abuse? And there's no sight of escaping it all. Everything is so mixed up and painful. It's ripping my heart out. Could it be that the Timeman has separated himself from darkness? And it's the light of the universe.

Even if this is true, he can't touch the world of the terror of the deep. He's powerless there. But again, the Timeman is the master of this universe, and here I live. I'll be homeless eternally! How could it be that I'm a curse to my ancestors? I can't accept this. The terror under the sea had saved me, so the totality of darkness can't be abolished. Maybe it's still sleeping in the deep. It's waiting to be awakened. Perhaps, there's some hope for me after all.

'If he's truly the Timeman, he should be able to see the future. But, how can the future be the future of the future?' He waited for an answer to come forth.

'For all time, get it straight,' cried the Timeman in Mr Cougar's waking state, 'there's only me. I'm the future of all conceivable futures. It's me who separated all things and gave each one of them a unique identity.' He departed as he appeared, and Mr Cougar looked around him to see whether others had heard the Timeman's voice.

Mr Cougar wanted him to pop up into his conscious state, because his surrounding could easily distract the Timeman. For he had to overcome the Timeman's reality. His face hanged with distress, for he would disappoint others more than himself. He could not see a way to bypass his ultimate tormentor, a gloated malevolent adversary in any world. He knew he had to be more cunning to slip past his dreadful opponent. He noticed that others in the room wore their sad, troubled faces, as though they had seen his failure. His confidence and internal power grew a little, for to overpowering that awesome creature had just started. He looked around at the journalists who were questioning people from his community.

Edwin appeared to be sedated under the spell of the Timeman's cosmos. He hadn't been prepared to witness how creation began. He admitted to himself that the Timeman emerged from the life source of everything. Edwin murmured, 'It is inconceivable to escape time. I've never been so confused in my life.'

'Perplexed, you mean.'

'I'm not certain whether I know your nature better than my grandpa's. For sure, my grandpa can't die. And yet, I can't understand how reincarnation takes place without anybody dying.'

'Every human is kept alive in my time cells. And if you're referring to me, it's called renewal.'

'You didn't see the coming of my grandpa before his birth. You won't allow my grandpa to die because he represents the renewal of creation. Everything will be different. It's like we can have a restart of how to live with everything on earth. Perhaps, my grandpa will free everyone from the time cells. He'll preserve community soul. Timeman, for some reason, you're self-ordained to undergo this renewal.'

'You're beginning to understand your nature, too.'

'For you everything is uncertain because you don't know whether or not the goddess will allow my grandpa to die. And if she does, this implies the extermination of your own nature, time. I hope she rejects my grandpa's wish. Because this is the only way that community soul can survive along with time.'

'I know that you won't be frightened about what you have witnessed. You understand your role in all this.'

'Are you telling me that my grandpa found his destiny in Sandreef but mine is elsewhere? And I've failed to help my grandpa? And his destiny is beyond my control, Timeman?' Had Edwin been reunited with his body, nothing could have stopped his tears.

'No, it isn't. A wish, you have. You could wish for my disappearance.'

'I won't exercise that wish. I think it is better for me to be reunited with my body. And in my quest, I'll remember community soul, especially how much he meant to me.'

'Your grandpa hasn't given up his struggle yet. His mother's flame still burns in him,' commented the Timeman, as he was reuniting Edwin's consciousness with his body.

15:45 Betty's love

Betty's family members and some neighbors were in Mr Cougar's bedroom. Most of them were standing while a handful of them were sitting on the floor. Betty appeared completely exhausted and weak from her ordeal, and her hair covered her face preventing a clear view. Mrs Potter, an older woman, was resting on her knees, and Betty leaned against her in a half sitting position. Mrs Potter held a damp handkerchief to Betty's forehead, and her caring was the best medicine for fatigue and exhaustion. Betty seemed to recover from her fainting spell, and she pushed Mrs Potter's hand away. The nail polish remover on the handkerchief seemed to have done its job, for it was used as the most effective substance to combat epileptic seizures, mild unconsciousness, and comas. Mrs Potter damped the cloth one more time in the bowl and added a few extra drops on it to create an overdose effect that would render Betty unconscious. 'Stop it!' cried Betty, pushing the cloth away from Mrs Potter's hand. Betty combed her hair away from her face with her hands, exposing her reddish forehead and swollen face. Several black lines of mascara ran down her face. Everyone giggled inwardly because she looked like a witch. She stared at everyone with her big and round eyes and noticed that her own family members were grinning at her. Her husband and son were too weak to interfere with neighborhood caring.

'Please, Betty. Stay here, my dear child. Stay with us. It's better for you. Your health, Betty. You've suffered too much!' comforted Mrs Potter.

'Yes, Betty-darling, listen to Dorothy,' asked her husband, Bradley, politely. She stared at him with dismay. Her facial muscles contracted in readiness; at last she realized that her husband was the big brain behind her family. He was trying very hard to keep her away from her father and sister and called her father the most unthinkable name. He believed that Betty should be the sole inheritor of the house, not her little sister.

'Yes, Mr Bradley, I know your type. You're trying to keep me away from his dying bed, my own father. How dare you?' Betty screamed very loud. Everyone in the living room heard her. This caused Mrs Potter to step back from family affairs, and she knew that this kind of overtone sang in everyone's house. She handed Betty a handful of Kleenex for her to wipe her running cosmetics. Before she confronted everyone in the living room, Betty cleaned her face and tried to look charming. Knowing that nothing could impede her from her quest, everyone stood aside while she struggled to stand up. She staggered back and forth on her legs. A few people near her made attempts to catch her if she fell. Finally, she regained her balance and then straightened out her clothes the best she could under the circumstances. She looked around for her purse and hairbrush but quickly forgot what she was looking for. Looking weaker and more drained than she was, she passed her hands over her face like a dramatist taking on a new role. She took a few wobbling steps without bumping into anyone, and then she stopped as though she had forgotten something.

Just before opening the door, she cried out like an opera singer, 'Oh, Ralph! How could you do it to me? A silence rushed in the house. For a long time mourners were waiting for someone to manifest their love and despair overtly. Betty was ready to display how her love for her father was measurable again. She had always embraced *King Lear* as the best drama ever written. Now she had the change to put love and death as a series of observable action. She slammed both hands on her chest and threw them widely apart to form a horizontal line. And then she brought them back to her chest. She repeated that action and then flung her hands over her head this time like an injured animal which staggered all over the place without hitting the floor. She hoarsely cried, 'How? How could you do this to your poor princess? Ooh, God, I'm gonna die! Oh, Ralph! Oh my Daddy! How could you leave your dearest daughter in this cruel world all alone? All alone in this dark and horrible world! Oh, Dad, I want to be in your place. I want to die a thousand deaths for you. Send me to the highest mountain dad and I'll get the flower of life for you. Please, Dad, don't go! Let me go for you! How could you leave poor Betty in this huge world?' As she threw her hands out in the air again, she actually lost her balance. Two bystanders caught her and held her upright. She kept them busy with about seventy percent of her bodily weight on their shoulders. The entire room was taken in by Betty's sentiment.

She continued again like an opera singer and the agony of lost love: 'Ooh, Dad! How could you? Leaving your loving daughter like this! How can I live a half-life? I can't endure this pain anymore! One half of me is already dead....' With some effort, she managed to drag her two helpers with her toward her father, as she was removing her hands from their shoulders and pushing them onto Lewis and Janet. Lewis abandoned his chair next to the bed and stood behind Betty. She embraced her father and then buried her face next to his. The mourners in the living room wept some more. 'Dad, I love you! And your love is the flame of my life,' she said loud enough for others to hear, and it moved all the nails on the wall. He tried to hold her as she sobbed all over him,, but he could not lift his hand. She started to stroke his gray hair gently.

'Betty, Betty. My dear child. I couldn't love you any less than your sister,' he softly murmured.

'Oh, Dad! You're my light in this world. Take me with you!'

He felt deeply sorry for himself, for he had neglected his older daughter without fully realizing it. 'Betty, I've tried to show you my fatherly love. But you could hardly stand still to see it. My dear child, whenever I tried to be near you, you jumped further away. Look at your sister, she looks harder than a stone. She couldn't cry or laugh. You are her inside. It takes two loving daughters to get the inside to match the outside. My dear Betty, bring your younger sister to me.' He glanced at the clock on the wall.

Betty stopped crying immediately; without any assistance, she went up to her sister: 'Come with me! How can you sit like that as though you've a heart of stone? How can you be so insensitive to your own father's anguish? You allow him to lie all alone in his dying bed without any comfort! Please, show him some mercy!' she cried for everyone to hear. Feeling bashful among the mourners, Catherine stood up at once, and Betty led her by the hand to his bed. Betty returned to her regular seat like a faithful daughter.

'Catherine, what have I done to my younger daughter? The last thing I'd ever wanted was to hurt my dearest children.'

'Oh, Dad! Please don't die,' cried Betty, holding her chest as though she was praying for him. She glanced around in the room, and she saw most mourners held their chests, too. Miss Cook gave her a sign to come, and Betty could not allow this change to pass by.

'Give me your hand dear child,' Cougar moved his right hand slightly under the blanket. Catherine passed her hand under the bed sheet. 'There's something, I have to do by myself. I need your strength to carry me on that path. Accept me, as I am,' he tried to reach Catherine's eyes without success. She contemplated his bony hand and fingers.

Her heart was burning up, and she was shouting for God to help her out of her confusion. She wanted to know what evil had taken over her father. She knew that her father did not smell like a corpse, but her intuition told her that death was near. And yet, he was too much alive to be a candidate for death.

Catherine's bewilderment drove her speechless for a while. When she had the urge to say something, her mouth was dryer than a desert. She glanced over at her sister who was speaking to the reporter. Interviewers had taken advantage of Betty on their program. They considered her as a remarkable speaker who put love on a digital scale.

Catherine felt at ease: 'If you succeed, I'd hold my head high, with glory and pride. Yes, Dad, the world will cherish your dignity, your honor, and pity your death. Everybody will tell me in the street, what a wonderful human being you are. And if you fail, I'll wear an old fishing basket over my head for the rest of my life. I wouldn't want to hear how degrading, shameful, dishonorable you're to your family, and to the entire community. Why do you want to make us rotten rubbish? Is that how you want your family to live?'

Mr Cougar realized his death would be very painful for his daughters. And their feelings of joy and pain hung on a pendulum. Catherine tightened her grip around his hand for some understanding and consideration, because her emotions and pain could not be easily burst out in the open for others to scrutinize.

'Dad, I haven't outgrown the golden beach. I'm still Mom's evening police. I'm the same little girl in the fishing boat in all kinds of weather. The little girl only gets older. And each of those images is precious for me. They're so rare and authentic. You make my life so priceless, Dad! And the fear of losing all this forever is a horror. You're robbing me of my roots, my self-worth, and my decency,' she whispered. She rechecked herself for a moment, for she thought of herself as someone who might forgive him had he been sick and suffering terribly in his dying bed.

'My child, my death won't be painless,' he said, showing humility in his eyes, as though he had been profoundly affected by his own dreadful situation. He did not want anybody to interrogate him further, for he was preparing himself for the journey. And Catherine's revelation added another chip onto his shoulder. He whispered to her: 'Our ancestors have abandoned me. Now, you don't believe in me. The Timeman has given us time, so we can live our lives fully. And to permit him to live in you would be an eternal curse. He'd be in your every breath, in every dream... I've left myself open for everybody to look inside.' He continued to mumble until his weak voice slowly disappeared.

As he slipped into a subconscious sleep, everyone eyed the monitors and the clock. Although the machines did not show any significant change, Dr Robinson moved quickly to recheck his pulse.

'How much have you convinced yourself that you could escape me,' cried the Timeman. 'Death, you don't want to tell your daughters about! How unworthy you are! You didn't tell them that!'

Recognizing his condition as being transparent before the Timeman, he subconsciously shifted to: 'Death, you can't control!'

'Look how broken-hearted, you've become. Your Nordic spirit has been sealed in one of my time cell for eternity. And they glorify their memories of conquering. Death could be eternal happiness or suffering, it all depends on your last conscious thought. You didn't tell your children how you want to hide from eternity. Struggling eternally to escape me, I could box you up in that very image! Meaningless efforts, you want me to eternalize. How could you wish for your fruitless efforts and wretched egoistic battle against me to stand out timelessly? You can't run away from your ultimate destiny. You'll be crumbled!'

'Never, Timeman! Empty hearted, I won't leave all these people. Never will I deceive my fellow beings. To home alone, I won't send them. Deceptive plan, I've none. For their forgiveness, I won't ask them. Without losing face and pride, they could easily forgive me. Yes, I know your iron arm is ticking away. The last breath of you, I haven't tasted yet.'

'In two and a half minutes, the clown of all clowns will be exposed.'

'Your name, my ancestors sung out and you obeyed. Me, they've forgiven. Can't you see how young I was to follow their steps. And yet, disgrace and dishonor couldn't have come from me. Never in your time cell, I'd live!'

'You're a good laugh. I'm sorry to see meaningless struggles,' enjoyed the Timeman, as Mr Cougar was about to admit his defeat.

'At first how convinced of myself, I was. So many doubts in me, you've awakened. All this uncertainty, I've to endure. Tears and disappointment in every heart, I see. To escape your domain, I cannot. A stubborn fool, I've been. You stand and work over all things with your power. With your spirit, everything is combed into place.'

'You should go and attend to your daughters and grandchildren. Catherine doesn't have to see a hairdresser. She doesn't need a face-lift. You've brought all this misery to your family because you want to will the future.' The Timeman faded away from his mind. Mr Cougar slowly opened his eyes. Catherine was still cresting his arm without irritating his fragile skin. They exchanged a quick glance and a polite smile. The recognition of parental love was reestablished. With his eyes he searched the room for Betty; he could hear her voice over everything else in the room.

A headliner without Betty's picture would be high treason. Her temperament expressed the right ingredient for the occasion, for nobody else in the room could display the emotion of bitter loss, the despair of death, and the distress that loved ones had to endure. Betty's solo was overwhelming; she could drift with any tide and harmonize with its flow. She behaved as thought she was convinced of her father's dying, and that she was experiencing it first hand.

Mr Cougar tried to stop his self-introspection, because whatever occurred to him was unfolding in the Timeman's domain. And yet, he could not repel the thought of his older daughter as being natural in any season. Unlike Catherine, Betty's seasons unfolded before him, and they could be foretold. He thought of Catherine as working too hard, and getting easily confused. It was more like the Timeman had controlled her will and destiny. He did not want to think that Catherine was working for the lord of time, but this thought grew stronger in him until he stared at Catherine: 'Against one of my daughters, the Timeman wants me to go,' he thought. He tried to move his hand away from hers, but he was too weak to move it. 'My hand, I can't move. Timeman's helper, she is to be!'

He knew he always had a special relationship with Catherine, and that he could tell her his dearest secrets. She would protect them. He thought again that all this time he had misjudged her honesty. He could not believe himself that he'd taken his most treacherous daughter for the honest one. Realizing how he had deceived himself, his hope disappeared. He knew that it was just too late to turn back the clock, and he wanted Betty to be near him for comfort.

'Why didn't the Timeman tell him about his deception? Perhaps, he did, but I didn't listen to him correctly.'

Catherine felt that his father was trying to hide himself from her, so she took a glance at him. That was enough to tell her that he looked very troubled, and she had never seen him like this before.

She also sensed he had a certain resentment toward her. But she could not leave him now, for everyone waited patiently to judge and condemn her. She knew that she had failed to show her love for him as well as Betty had done. She thought about Betty: that she'd used her father for her own egocentric life style.

Mr Cougar closed his eyes to avoid seeing Catherine; he felt that he hated her. She did not have one tear for him, and the only thing she could do was to hide herself in the corner, and hide her phoniness. He said to himself: 'Thanks, for showing me her true nature. She couldn't have deceived me forever. And still, I couldn't curse her away from me. She'd always be my daughter.' He opened his eyes and grumbled incomprehensibly: 'Oh, no! What am I doing to myself? All I could see before me were only conflicts. I'm having layers of doubt! Oh, my Betty, you're a swimmer in any weather. Oh, my precious daughter, you hide your true love for me.'

Catherine checked the monitors to confirm her beliefs, and then the clock: 'It's two to four. Only two minutes left,' she thought, staring at him and then closing her eyes. She thought about how many things she wanted to tell him.

Her thoughts wandered again, and she cried: 'Where is Edwin? He should be here! Where is he? He's gone, now! Why does he do this to me?' Mr Cougar overheard her bewildered cry.

While she was absentminded for that split second, her mind was synchronized with her father's. They both heard a humming voice coming from the shore, and it was becoming more distinct. 'Stand strong!' Edwin spoke to them in a dream. 'The Timeman saw the future, so he came to change it. Then, he saw his failure, so he came to change that too. He had seen his failure again and again. For all time, he could only see his failure until his failure runs infinitely.' Then his voice disappeared, as quickly as it had appeared.

Catherine stared at her father for an explanation. His hand grasped her tightly until he felt her forgiveness. Mr Cougar realized that Edwin could not come to his aid directly, but he could do it through his mother because the door was open for Catherine. Catherine was still staring at him as though she was in a daze, for all this was much bigger than she could have imagined. Her heart gradually lost its heaviness and darkness, as she believed that the golden body she'd seen playing off the sandy shore when she was a child was much more than a mortal. And yet, she couldn't understand what Edwin was saying. The meaning of his words surpassed her understanding. Her heart appeared to stop when she saw the last minute coming to play its tone in the wind.

16:00 The Community is Life

In the house, Mr Cougar took a quick look at the clock when he felt Catherine's assuring hand and saw Betty coming over, too. The mourners were still, as the ticking clock became louder and louder. It appeared to hypnotize everyone internally as they witnessed that the art of dying was found in living, having time for love, growing lovingly, and respecting life for what it's worth. Lewis held Janet's hand; Dr Robinson grabbed the bed edge tightly. Miss Cook was observing everybody else: Keith and his friends coming in, and Richard and Betty's family standing closer to the bed. And yet, she was thinking how people would see Mr Cougar. She thought that Mr Cougar would always be in people's hearts.

Most international calls from foreign government offices to the Prime Ministry of Canada had already been made, and friendly political leaders expressed their deep respect and condolences on behalf of their nations. People of the world saw Mr Cougar's dying as a heroic endeavor of how to live. And living could not be less than the art of making as many friends as possible, and that surpassed any borders. In praising Mr Cougar as a model for human beings, everyone believed in his victory over darkness and torture that overshadows life. And people were ready to honor his victory as one that would be remembered for a long time.

Miss Cook commented to her audience: 'If Mr Cougar has lost his battle, we should be reminded that he had fought against an invincible adversary. And not being able to conquer death tells us about the sweetness of being alive and enjoying it lovingly.

'Sandreef has transformed the world by reminding people of their isolation, loneliness, and the meaning of life and death. With technology to bring people closer together, they may still run away from love and genuine friendship. Mr Cougar's accomplishment in life shows that he's neither a winner nor a loser. And yet, a community in humans burns deeper than anything else. And his flame of life can't die a loving death.' Suddenly, Miss Cook braced herself against the wall for security.

The north wind swept across the ocean and the song of how to die simply hissed as the secret of living. Scotty was not sure if he heard the wind singing, so he glanced at Edwin for an acknowledgement of that peculiar phenomenon. Edwin ignored him and attended to the countdown. He knew that his grandfather would not reveal all of his secrets to anyone, for he had prepared himself to undertake the ultimate battle without any doubts in his mind. He did not know what manner it would take against the Timeman. He thought that because others believed in him, it would bring his final victory. His mother identified herself with his grandpa, and that relationship could have brought about his defeat. For his mother's love was drawing him away from death. At last, she accepted the fact that Grandpa had to go.

'And for me, I don't think I've any misguided beliefs about my grandpa. He taught me well about how to mold my destiny. It's like a knitting a fishing net—eye by eye in perfect harmony, putting my heart at ease,' thought Edwin.

All joined in the countdown. As the last second ticked, Mr Cougar closed his eyes and the monitors stopped. Dr Robinson found no pulse rate or heartbeat. The doctors from upstairs came quickly and reaffirmed Dr Robinson's verdict. All onlookers felt as thought they'd swallowed hot dumplings that would burn for a long time to come.

Edwin and Scotty were still combing the horizon. They saw a thick white cloud coming toward them. And below it, a huge Viking ship was following the cloud. Next to the ship, a huge shark swam with it. *The terror of the sea and the terror of the deep are coming for my grandpa*, Edwin thought. They came very close to the shore and stopped, as though they were waiting for a passenger.

Scotty finally remembered why he started to drink and what caused his trances. He had tapped into Mr Cougar's treasure chest. One evening when he was walking on the beach, he had seen Mr Cougar riding a shark's back. Scotty had stared into the shark's eyes, and from then on, he was drawn into it, being trapped in a different dimension. He could not escape its gripping power. During his trances, he lived in the realm of the shark's eyes. Though he tried very hard to fight back by making himself drunk, he became an alcoholic.

Edwin and Scotty looked behind them for a passenger. With their amazement, they saw a huge icy face leaving Sandreef. It stopped and looked at them. Edwin felt a burning sensation on his chest. He still followed the face as it went between the shark and the ship and embraced them closely. As both the Viking ship and the shark were about to disappear on the horizon, the icy face took refuge in the cloud and vanished just like the shark and the Viking ship.

Edwin rubbed his eyes with disbelief, and then he examined why he had a burning sensation on his chest. It occurred where the medallion was hanging. When he touched the medallion, he felt the birth of love lashing away for a split second and then it disappeared. Without speaking to each other, Edwin and Scotty rushed back quickly to the house. Because of Scotty's obnoxious smell, they easily got to the house. They had a shock when they saw the face in the sky was identical to the one lying in Mr Cougar's bed. They looked at each other, and then both of them raised their eyebrows in bewilderment. They stood there without knowing what to say; they settled with looking at the mourners' single line to the bed; they came and touched Mr Cougar's bed sheet and then left peacefully. Edwin went to his mother and whispered into her ear, 'Grandpa wished to be cremated and then to have his ashes scattered in the ocean.'

Epilogue

I really thought about how I want others to remember me. And I would like to know all of my friends very well. I have also put down my defenses and mask to allow others to enter into my life. I can't say all this for Edwin. He left Sandreef two weeks after everything actually happened. I believe that he had gone to the south seas.